In Search Of

Aditi Bathia

Leadstart
INKSTATE

ISBN 978-93-5438-717-3
Copyright © Aditi Bathia, 2021

First published in India 2021 by Inkstate Books
An imprint of Leadstart Publishing Pvt Ltd

Sales Office:
119-123, 1st Floor, Building J2, B - Wing,
Wadala Truck Terminal, Wadala East,
Mumbai 400022, Maharashtra, INDIA
Phone: +91 96999 33000
Email: info@leadstartcorp.com
www.leadstartcorp.com

Disclaimer: The views expressed in this book are those of the Author and do not pertain to be held by the Publisher.

Editor: Cora Bhatia
Cover: Shrinivas Rao
Layouts: Kshitij Dhawale

To Saisha and Pluto

ABOUT THE AUTHOR

Aditi Bathia is an insights consultant by profession, currently employed with a leading management-consulting firm, who loves uncovering peoples' said and unsaid intentions and emotions. A new mother and a dog parent, she is currently juggling parenthood with work, while trying to find time to pursue her passion – writing. Being an ardent traveller, Aditi picks up the essence of her stories from the several people and places she encounters when on the go. She loves to sketch strong characters in her stories, reflecting the underlying feminist within her.

'In Search Of' is her debut novel.

Contact Info:

Aditi Bathia

Aditi.h.bathia@gmail.com

+91 9820437233

LinkedIn: https://www.linkedin.com/in/aditi-bathia-69925a16/

Twitter: @aditibathia

ACKNOWLEDGEMENTS

Ihad always dreamt of writing my own book ever since the magic of reading laid its charm on me. Today, this dream has come true, and it is only because of the immense support, motivation, and encouragement I received from my near and dear ones.

Let me firstly thank my husband – Rajdip Banerjee. This book would not have been in your hands today had he not pushed me to strive to achieve my dreams. Thank you for reading and re-reading the manuscript until you were satisfied about what this could turn out to be. You made sure I stayed focussed, took care of the baby, so I could take the time out to write, and most importantly, believed in me. You made this happen. This book is as much yours as it is mine.

I would also like to thank my sister – Dr. Kairavi Gokani for her endless suggestions, even in the midst of a crazy day at her clinic. Your enthusiasm is infectious. I love you!

Next in line is the entire team at Leadstart Publishing for the constant support throughout. I would like to thank my manager Ananya, and my editor Cora for guiding me along the right path. Thank you for making this dream come true.

Now, I need to thank two most important people – one who introduced me to the world of books, who taught me to fall in love with stories, and who believed I was capable of achieving anything I dreamt of; and the other who challenged me and my knowledge at every step so I could be the best version of myself. Thank you, Mom and Dad. This book is for you.

The soul searches for peace within,

Unstirred by the chaos

That the heart has caused

By its vileness, unfaithfulness, foolishness;

Unfettered by the frailties

That love has brought along

With its coyness, shyness, shrewdness;

Undeterred by the pain

That the heart suffers

For its carelessness, silliness, mindlessness;

Unprepared to succumb to the loss

That lapses in sanity have bred

Through thoughtlessness, senselessness, recklessness...

The silly soul searches for peace,

Unaware of the damage done,

Its permanency, incurability, mortality.

PROLOGUE

Dearest Aarav,

I hope this mail finds you in good health. I know it is no longer fashionable to write long letters, but you know I am not good with sharing my feelings out loud. And so, I burden you with the task of reading a long, possibly even poorly structured, monologue that I am sharing with you.

I know I have not been fair to you on more than one occasion. Therefore, I felt it was important to let you know of my reasons behind the choices I made. With this letter, you will find the diary I wrote in the past few months, hoping to share with you someday; all that I was unable to tell you during our time together.

Perhaps, I am selfish in this as I hope for you to understand my *love* for you and *me* a little better with this. I want you to know that with this diary, I am lending you a piece of my heart – the same that had loved you beyond measure. I hope you read it well.

Love,

Anya

PROLOGUE

Dearest Yohan,

I hope this mail finds you in good health. I know it is no longer fashionable to write long letters, but you know I am not good with sharing my feelings out loud. And so, I burden you one last time with the task of reading a long, possibly even poorly structured, monologue that I am sharing with you.

I know I have not been fair to you on more than one occasion. Therefore, I felt it was important to let you know of my reasons behind the choices I made. With this letter, you will find the diary I wrote in the past few months, hoping to share with you someday; all that I was unable to tell you during our time together.

Perhaps, I am selfish in this for I hope for you to understand me a little better with this. I want you to know that with this diary, I am lending you a piece of my heart – the same that had cared for you beyond measure. I hope you read it well.

Love,

Anya

MOMENTS

Dearest Aarav,

Magic.

That is what we humans live for – to find magic in our mundane lives. We strive to seek magic all around us (as if it will give a purpose to our lives) – in a baby's laughter, in the mystic of nature, in the notes of a melody, in love. Perhaps that is why we strive so hard to find love, and strive to find it ever so often, so that we can have magic in our arms whenever we desire. In a way, finding love makes finding magic easier.

Love – a magic unlike any other. One whence anxiety and excitement makes you lose all sense of self and surroundings. The butterflies in your stomach refuse to settle down, and your heart discovers a shy awkwardness for the first time. Daydreams haunt you in the day and sleeplessness fills your nights. Amidst all this, a soft, pleasing smile is plastered to your face for no apparent reason! The bliss is incomparable to anything else.

I was fortunate to have felt all of this the first time we met. A seemingly normal party of a seemingly normal bunch of youngsters, at a seemingly normal pub. Except, what seemed like a normal conversation between two strangers was unlike any other conversation they had had with anybody, ever. Two regular young adults surrounded by an entire group of friends, some familiar, some new, yet feeling awkwardly lost in the crowd, somehow fitting perfectly with each other, like two pieces of a jigsaw puzzle. There was magic, right there – in that evening, in that conversation, in our eyes. Yes, it was just the first time, and no, I did not believe in love at first sight. But there it was – finding me in the most unexpected moment, consuming me with all its power, leaving me dazed in its spell for long after it was gone, or so I thought.

I felt all of these topsy-turvy set of emotions once again when we met that day, eight years later. Yes, eight years had passed since we had last met, and no, life was not the same now. Yet, there I was, smitten by your charm, losing myself slowly, but consciously, in your dimpled smile and almond eyes that peeked innocently from behind those rimless spectacles, all over again. No, I did not fall for your hotshot looks, although your six-foot frame, and broad shoulders, did help the cause. But I do think it was your warmth that did the magic. Your smile set me at ease and your deep voice was so comforting, yet it burned my core with desire so strong, I was willing to commit adultery with complete knowledge.

Yes, adultery it was, for wasn't I bound by vows to be loyal to my man for seven lives – with my body, mind and soul? At least that is what we had supposedly signed up for when he had put that ring on my finger five years ago. Five years! Here I am talking about eternity, when even five years was making marriage feel like a constant struggle to me. I won't say I was unhappy. There wasn't any particular issue between us either. In fact, I am sure my husband and I came across as an ideal couple to many an outsider when they met us. Perhaps, it was just the lack of love. No that might be a very strong judgment to pass, for who am I to understand the meaning of something that many a mighty poet has failed to fathom! Neither was it just lack of spark, or even understanding. Perhaps, it was just that phase when you become too comfortable with someone to feel any excitement any longer. Yes, perhaps it was just that – lack of excitement, boredom even. Or perhaps, it was something more?

But you seemed to promise answers to all those looming questions...

Yes you, with your deep, gazing look that defied any restraint. You had cast a spell on me the very first day we had met, and you did it again that day in that meeting room. And I knew you were smitten too. I knew, because I had noticed your look that lingered on me just a tad longer. That handshake that you held for an extra second. And that slightly long pause you took after the goodbyes were said, hoping to not end the moment, trying to figure out a sensible thing to say to not let go of that moment – our moment – and, and yet make it seem normal.

But no, normal it was not.

Normalcy does not allow impulsiveness. Normalcy does not fumble during a formal chat over a cup of coffee with a client. Normalcy does not grant the right to a married woman to be carried away in the moment. So no, it was not normal. Yet, it felt that way, didn't it?

It felt so normal to me to break the norms and accept an invitation for dinner with you – my client – knowing all too well that no work was going to be discussed over it. I remember making an excuse at home that day – the first of many to come – about an office event I had forgotten to mention about. I remember trying on five different outfits and rejecting them all for not making me look perfect for you (I won't deny having put in some good effort over the years in maintaining my petite construct, although, I must admit I settled on a tight number so you I could flaunt it to you). I remember putting on a darker shade of lipstick than I normally did, so my lips could look fuller to you. I remember putting on high heels that night to elevate my tiny five-foot-five frame. And I remember leaving my short curls untied, just the way you used to like them.

And, I also remember packing a toothbrush, just in case.

I remember all this, and I remember finding it very normal, almost as if it was routine for me to do this – to take a chance at being carried away.

The only thing that defied the normalcy was the giddiness in my stomach. I wasn't naïve to not know that I was overstepping my boundaries. In fact, it was just the opposite. I knew that the moment I stepped out of the house in that little red dress, I was hitting the start button to something very dangerous and irreversible.

Yet, I was unable to stop myself from being drawn to you. You had cast that kind of magic on me!

My mind drew itself back to the time when we had been inseparable…

That day, a decade ago, when you smiled at me from a distance, noticing how awkward I was feeling in the (kind of a loud) party I had not been used to back then. You then walked over to me to strike small talk, only to admit how lost you yourself were feeling. We laughed over your shy admittance and got talking. And then talking some more, and then a little more – until people started leaving and we realized we had spent the entire evening with just each other. After the party, you had offered to drop me home. A mere half hour drive from the place in Khar to my house in Andheri, but we chose to take a detour to the beach along the way. The quiet air of the late hour made the beach distance itself from the chaotic Mumbai city that never slept. In that distance, we created a space for ourselves – me in your arms, and you in mine. In that space, we kissed for the first time – a soft, reluctant touch that seemed to be coming from a different world. In that world, we found our love – a love that grew deeper with each passing day, until fate got envious and bit us with its venomous fangs.

A shudder ran through me thinking of that time when we had to part ways and sprang me back to the present. The present where we had just met once again – eight long years later.

I won't lie about being nervous about the meeting earlier that morning ever since I had read your name on the meeting invite. The meeting was to be an official one, where you (or rather your firm) were to be my firm's client, and the one where we (my boss, myself and the rest of my team) were to meet you and your team to offer you our services for your brand's new ad campaign. I had wondered if it would be awkward seeing you after so long. Had you also noticed my mention in the invite? Would you care when we met, or would you deliberately act indifferent? How would we deal with our past?

But your composed stance that morning had given me a good dose of professionalism. It was then that I knew I would be able to deal with this project without letting our personal biases meddle in our professional conduct. That was, until you came up with the invite for the dinner, of course.

Do you remember that first dinner? Of course, you do. How could you forget the candle lit table in the cozy corner of Escobar Lounge? You had been waiting for me at the entrance, like a true gentleman that you were – dressed in an indigo blue casual shirt and dark grey chinos. I noticed you eyeing me as I stepped out of my car, and I knew you seemed pleased with what you saw. For some reason, it seemed like old times, but of course, it was unlike any other time. Times had changed, I had married and probably you had as well!

I felt stupid to have not thought of this earlier. Possibly, you genuinely just wanted to catch up, and I let myself be carried away with all this imagination in my head…

Recovering my composure, I put on my guard and initiated the cordialities. Of course, it was supremely awkward at first, being there, on a dinner date with you, after all these years. Soon, you took charge of the conversation and put me at ease with that warm, comforting smile.

"So, how is married life treating you?" you asked suddenly. I wondered for a moment how you had assumed that, but I realized it was probably the ring.

"As it treats everyone after a few years," I replied with a smile, but I could not meet your eyes, afraid you might notice the emptiness.

"I hope to God you are happy, so at least, I know letting you go was worthwhile," you said, matter-of-factly. What could I have said to this? That yes, I live what one might say is an ideal marriage, and yet I have thought of you every day since the day we parted? I had no answer for you, so I shifted the topic to you.

"What about you? Wife, kids?" I asked, almost innocently.

"Hah!" you smirked tauntingly. "I did not find moving on as easy as you. So, I had to bury myself in work to keep you out of my head. Before I knew it, I got used to being on my own," you shrugged. "In fact, I started liking my independence quite a bit. Marriage did not cross my mind again, and I plan on keeping it that way."

I sensed the bitterness in what you said, and in your eyes that pierced their gaze right through me. But I could not blame you. We hadn't parted on exactly amiable terms. In fact, I found myself getting back at you with a sharp one, "You and your work, I hope to God you are rich, so at least I know letting you go was worthwhile."

I regretted those words as soon as I uttered them. But of course, it was too late. You were going to give it back to me, and I was willing to take the strike.

Except, you just laughed lightly and said, "You haven't changed one bit!" And raised your glass of sparkling wine to a toast, "To old times!"

And just like that, you averted a sour turn to take a spicy one. I say spicy because of what you said next, "In fact, if I may add, you still look just as hot," and winked as you took a sip of your wine.

Deny as I might, I felt my cheeks go hot when I heard you say that. "You don't look too bad yourself," I found myself saying, putting away an unruly twig of my curls behind the ear, picturing your well-toned body beneath the slim-fit shirt you had donned, and raised my own glass to you and laughed away the bitterness with you. The awkwardness was slowly receding; giving way to – shall I say – flirtatiousness? I should have felt guilty then, but I pushed away whatever the conscious voice in my head was telling me, to make way for the moment to take over.

We ordered Chicken Kiev and Spaghetti in Pesto (wasn't it delicious?) and caught up on life as we chatted away. I apologized for my earlier snarky comment, and you, humble as ever, shrugged it off. You mentioned that you continued living in Toronto for your mom's treatment for over a year after we broke up, before moving to Singapore with Gainz Global Ltd. while your mom continued to live there with your brother and his wife. While in Singapore, you worked your way up the ranks from brand executive to brand manager and eventually category manager, growing the portfolio of the prominent FMCG brands you managed, leading to some of the well-known success stories in the market. You had only moved back to Mumbai six months ago, when E&M Foods had approached you with a challenging role to lead their declining foods portfolio. Unable to resist the challenge, you packed your bags and landed here, (as luck would have it) as my client!

"Didn't you feel the need for companionship over these years?" I finally asked you, unable to hold my curiosity any longer.

"You mean did I date anyone in all this time?" you smirked once again, reading my mind. "Of course, I dated a few women. A couple of them are still very good friends. But as I said, I was not looking to put a stamp on the relationship, so none of them lasted very long."

I must admit, I did feel the initial restlessness go away when you said this. I was surprised at how much impact your relationship status had on me!

A moment of quiet passed, and then you added, "To be honest, I kept looking for you in every woman I dated. I am not sure I could have loved anyone as much. I cannot tell you how much I regret my decision all those years ago. I shouldn't have let you go."

Your gaze was back on me, where I held it for a long moment, and in your eyes, I could see the same old love from all those years ago. It seemed as if nothing had changed. In that moment, we were back to our younger selves, the young Aarav and young Anya that had been so in love. In that moment, I won't deny, I was in love with you once again.

Perhaps that was why, when the cheese drooled down the

corner of my mouth, I let you wipe it off with your thumb. Very clichéd, but it worked. Everything you did, or did not, seemed to have worked. Wrong as it may seem, I was in a spell and had no desire to be rescued.

Just as I had no desire to free myself from your arms when you held me later. We were in your car and you had paused before turning on the ignition. I felt you turn towards me; hold my gaze for a bit before putting your arm around me. I felt you draw me closer, and saw you leaning in, until our lips touched. I can still feel the electric pulse it sent through my veins. I felt your passion course through your arms that were steadily moving up, through your mouth that just didn't seem to be getting enough.

You broke the hold after a bit; we both looked out of the window before looking back at each other in knowing silence. Quietly then, you turned on the ignition and we drove away.

That toothbrush was going to come in handy.

We drove in silence for all of the twenty minutes it took us to get to your apartment in Bandra. Once there, we did not need the formalities. The rush was too much to hold onto anymore, and it came gushing out with all the intensity of passion we could muster. You grabbed me the moment the door closed behind us, kissed me hard on the lips and all but literally tore my clothes off. I too could resist no more, and arched back to give you more of me, as my hands found the buttons of your shirt. Your bare chest closed in on me as we made our way to the bedroom, still kissing wildly. You flopped me down and got on top of me. Your lips found its way down to my neck, my shoulder blades, and my breasts. I moaned under the tingling sensation of your lips while guiding your hand up my thighs. You then unzipped your pants and let your passion unfold unto me, as my head reeled in a final wave of ecstasy. We moaned in pleasure that was better than either of us had anticipated – wild, steamy, sweaty, and sexy – better than any other time we had had it. It had to be that way; nothing less would've done.

✳ ✳ ✳

I think the first blow of reality hit me when I awoke the next morning in an unfamiliar room. As the previous night's memory came rushing, the overwhelming feeling of guilt quickly turned to fear and eventually panic. My first instinct was to get up and leave as quickly and quietly as possible. I started to pick up my belongings, and just as I turned to leave, my sight fell upon my reflection in your bedroom mirror. The woman staring back seemed a stranger to me. She made me feel cheap and dirty. I tried to look away, but just then, you stirred from your slumber. I couldn't help but admire the tiny smile you had on your sleepy face. You appeared so completely at peace.

You woke up just as I was having these thoughts running through my head. When your eyes opened up to me, there was no surprise on your face, or awkwardness in your stance. I recall wondering if you realized the wrong in our actions, but you simply called me over with the sweet smile of yours, unaffected by any defied norms. And just like that, looking into your eyes, all of my panic vanished away...

We spent a lazy morning indoors. You offered making us breakfast and I decided to freshen up in the meantime. I noticed how masculine your house actually was, with its dark-wood furniture and leather upholstery, wooden floor and the typical boys-gadget collection (of course, you had to have a smart house!) I noticed the lack of any personal touches though. Walking across to the kitchen, I saw you fixing us a breakfast of coffee, omelet and toast. We relished it in bed while chatting away effortlessly, speaking about everything under the sun. It was somewhere between that cup of coffee and the chat that I saw a different side of you, a side that was soft at heart, so contrary to the front your house put up. You showed the same genuine interest in knowing about my life as you always did, and I opened up to you, as I had not to anyone else in a very long time. I let you know how I had been lost after you had left, taking over a year to get over you, but still being stuck somewhere in the past. And you buried me in your embrace to let me know you were back and would not let me go ever again. It did not surprise me that my marital status did not seem to bother either of us, though; looking back now, I do feel it would have helped matters if we had actually given it the due consideration it deserved.

The conversation flowed smoothly, and we lost all track of time. I realized I had to get back home before it was too late. I got up, slowly letting go of your hand, only realizing then that we had been holding it all this while. That simple gesture seemed like a tormentor's task. Unwillingly, we let our entwined fingers loose.

That, in that *un-entwining*, was the beginning of something more than a one-night stand, more than a short fling. That breakfast defined our relationship, metamorphosing it from vulgar adultery to something pure and true.

That, in that moment, was the beginning of 'us'.

GENESIS

Dearest Yohan,

One does not plan to fall in love. One does not plan to lose love, either. But the pain of losing love can destroy a person in unfathomable ways. Yet, even more unfathomable, is to find love for a second time.

My dear Yohan, one does not plan to be an infidel. And yet, when love presents itself to a married one, it destroys lives in ways unfathomable.

That first morning, I rehearsed my excuse all the way home. I was quite nervous. In fact, I was sure my demure was going to give me away. I reached home about noon, only to find you just about waking up from sleep.

"I took the liberty of sleeping on much longer today, since you weren't around to wake me up," you said teasingly on seeing me. You asked if I had fun and asked how Shyna was (I had told you I was staying over at hers). I was about to get on with my well-rehearsed answer, but just as I was about to speak, you walked away. Clearly, you had no interest in actually knowing about her, or my party for that matter. Your indifference bothered me a little. Not that I wanted you to doubt me, but a little interest and concern would not have harmed, would it? But then, you had always been this way. I had tried pointing it out to you in our early years, and you had shunned it away carelessly. It was your way of 'keeping life simple', you had justified back then. When I had pushed you, you chucked it again, saying you trusted me completely – both, that I could take care of myself and that I would never betray you – so there was no reason for you to worry. I wondered then, if you found your latter assumption had just gone down the drain, would you be affected at all, or would you simply find a new excuse to get on with life as if nothing significant had really happened, so you could keep life simple...

Such thoughts haunted me all day long. My mind was an amalgamation of emotions – feeling nervous, anxious, excited and angry all at once. The train of thoughts jumped from reminiscing the previous night with *him*, to recalling the journey of *our* five years of married life. One moment I was exhilarated by the thought of *his* touch on my bare skin last night, and the next moment I was angry for having put up with being ignored by *you* for so long. One moment I questioned my self-worth, the next I felt I had finally found a way to love myself once again. On one hand, I was worried about ruining our marriage, and on the other hand, I was upset at myself for tolerating an unsatisfying relationship for so long.

Unable to focus on the task at hand, I took a sidelong glance at you – my husband – and found you blithefully scrolling down some random article on your laptop. Had you not noticed anything different in me? The angst surfaced once again and made me question the entire journey of our marriage.

Surely, we had not been this way all along – why we had been the most compatible pair ever, on paper and otherwise! With your vivacious personality and double degree in management, along with a sound career in investment banking, you had marked all the ticks on my (and my parents') checklist. Probably, the same applied to you as well, for you found all you sought in your partner in me – good looks, a desire for success and a strong personality – or what you call as the quintessential woman of the twenty first century. We hit it off instantly when we met through the arranged set-up. Our parents thought we looked good together – you with your five-eight physique, short-straight hair, a rough stubble and a square jawline that highlighted your tiny but bright eyes, and me with my petite frame, curly hair and wheatish complexion to match yours. We, on the other hand, were more interested in our intellectual compatibility. So, we spent a long time talking about life goals and ways of life, which surprisingly seemed to align perfectly. It was indeed a perfect match!

The marital bliss continued for the initial couple of years with a ton of parties to attend and to host, the ample vacations and dining out; time flew by in a jiffy. Until gradually, the high wore off and routine took over. Even so, our pragmatism kept us good. We supported each other through stressful times in our respective careers and took care of each other in sickness (and in health – as the vows go). So, what was it then that drifted us apart? What was the missing link that broke the pace and parted our tracks? What caused the conversations change to discussions, sex to task and love to obligation?

The memories of the past five years flashed in front of me like a movie trailer, with all its drama elements – the hero and heroine meeting, the golden-period of dating, the wedding preparations, the elaborate ceremony, the romantic European honeymoon, the happy times, the high life, and the parties. Then (with the music turning tense in the background) the little disagreements, the little disappointments, the first major fight, and the first cancelled vacation. The gradually increasing heated arguments, the changing personalities, the seeping in of the seemingly harmless cordialities, the coldness, aloofness, and lovelessness.

One distinct incident kept recurring in the visuals my head was seeing. The day of our third anniversary and this time, after a lot of arm-wrestling, you were able to take a couple of days' leave from work and we had gone out on an extended weekend to Kerala to celebrate the occasion. Beautiful as the mountains of Munnar were, you had taken extra efforts to make the day more special, or shall I say more romantic! To be honest, the day did seem perfect with the scrumptious meal on the terrace of our villa, with the scenic tea gardens in the backdrop and the vivacious flower garden up ahead. The light rain had given way to the mist, which rose from the valley below, and gave the set-up a dreamy feel. How then did we end up having one of the nastiest fights of our marriage ever? How did we manage to bring up all the hidden frustrations and angst in the midst of such a beautiful setting?

If I remember correctly, it started with a small disagreement over dessert – we were given the wrong order and instead of arguing with the waiter, we started arguing amongst ourselves over whose fault it was, who always messes up the smallest of things, who needs to be more adjusting and who always ends up compromising. From there we went on to bringing in all the fringe elements into the brawl – including our career plans. We argued about how you had to give up moving to another city because of me, as if I were holding you back. We spoke about family planning (on why I was still not ready to have a baby even though we had been married for three years and were already in our thirties). And of course, we brought in our respective families into the fight as well (and as is a proven fact in the history of all relationships, families, especially in-laws, are always a shortcut to escalating matters). And so, escalate the fight did. Before we knew it, we had accused each other of being untrustworthy, un-giving and un-respectful. I accused you of being a selfish person who did not know how to give the slightest of attention or respect to his wife and her choices, and in return, I was accused of not being a good wife because I was not ready to bear you a child. These accusations crossed the unsaid boundary we had set in our relationship and left a scar on our marriage.

While the fight was resolved the next day, we had woken up changed people. We had both gained a few realizations that day. The first one was that we were both capable of getting very ugly should the need arise, and so we must simply avoid such situations from recurring if we wanted to maintain the peace in our marriage. As a result, we turned extra careful about picking on each other, especially on small matters. Looking back now, I feel it was this conscious decision that played a big role in bringing about aloofness between us. Afraid of provoking each other, we both started minding our own businesses, leaving the other alone to his own.

The second realization was that what seemed on the surface to be a great relationship actually had many underlying issues that had been left undealt for a very long time. Somehow, despite realizing this at that time, we chose not to act on the issue, as we knew any further discussion was an invitation to yet another outburst, which neither of us was ready to deal with. So, we let the issues be buried, and going forward, layered them further with many more problems that were neither discussed nor dealt with. Only later, I realized that having left these issues unattended was the primary cause of growing discontent and disdain between us, which eventually led to this marriage being bereft of any love.

I know that one fight sounds too trivial to affect a relationship for so long, I mean come on don't all couples fight? That's true. But I suppose because we were of such a similar temperament – alpha personalities as they say, we chose to ignore our problems. We did this to such a great degree that in order to not be bad to each other we ended up covering ourselves in a pretentious blanket of 'goody-good' when instead; we should have in fact faced the issues head on. In moments when we did have our outbursts, things turned so ugly that the only way we were able to resolve issues was by staying apart for a few days, until we were both ready to return to our pretentious selves.

I wish now that we had not acted the way we did back then. I wish we had learned to be more vulnerable, as I learned it the difficult way that it is only in your weaknesses that you become capable of trusting someone, and love cannot grow in the absence of trust. I wish we had tried harder to fight with each other – at least we would have been true to each other. I wish we had spoken out all that we chose to keep buried in our hearts – at least we would not have been burdened with the weight of those unsaid grudges. I wish we had tried harder to give each other second chances – then perhaps, we would not have been here today.

I wish I had tried harder. I know *I* should have tried harder.

Five years into marriage, we were still extremely cordial with each other, but perhaps not warm. Gone was the mutual care or concern we had held for each other in our initial years together, regardless of our disagreements. We still agreed with each other on most aspects, but perhaps, it was mostly to avoid a conflict. We still showed each other affection (and if I am to be honest, most of it was still genuine), but it was mostly because we had grown used to each other, not necessarily because we were in love with each other.

So then, where did that leave me on the infidelity score? Was

I indeed being disloyal to someone that I was no longer attached to? Or was I using this 'affair' with *him* as an excuse to vent out my frustration with my marriage? Was I, in that case, not being disloyal to *him* instead?

With these and a million other questions running through my head, I fell into a restless sleep.

MEMORIES

Dearest Aarav,

The next morning, I woke up with chaos in my mind. I panicked once again over the sin I had committed and ended up sweating profusely. I rushed into the shower hoping to get some respite. Instead, my mind only reminisced at the grief that losing you had caused several years ago…

"I have amazing news for us, Anya," you said excitedly. We had met at the Pizzeria on that Friday evening post work. I knew you were to have an important interview that day for a dream profile at the FMCG company you always wanted to work with – Gainz Global Ltd. So, amazing news implied you had cleared the interview. I could not have been more thrilled. The occasion called for celebration, but I thought of having some fun first. "Wait, wait. I am starving. Let's order our wood-fried pizza first," I said nonchalantly, "And also, I want to just use the washroom if you don't mind," and I got up from the table, taking my bag along, a sign that you were well aware of by now – that I would be taking longer freshening up. A look of restlessness passed over your face, but you controlled it well.

Ten minutes later, when I returned, you had started to get fidgety. "Now ma'am, may I have your attention to disclose the big news?

"Of course. Oh wait, I think I forgot to inform my boss that I have sent the presentation to the client in two parts. If he misses the second one, he will unnecessarily send out stinkers. Let me text him first?" I insisted, pressing you on the verge of an outburst. While it was fun to see your restlessness, I knew it would be a while before you lost your cool enough to begin yelling. And so, I had to invent more excuses to divert the topic for some more time…

"Thank goodness I messaged him. He replied saying he was about to call me to ask about the pending sections. I know him so well! He will never breathe easy, nor let others in the team rest well, even after office! I am sure everyone in the team has at least one nightmare of him every week," I said jovially, urging you to join me in my mock humour.

"Ha-ha. Yeah, he seems like a big pain in the arse. But listen, you won't believe what happened today…" you began once again.

"Oh yeah, talking of unbelievable – you know that Rishi Malhotra – our VP Marketing? Would you believe if I told you that he just got married, again? I wonder where he finds all these eligible girls to marry again and again! This is his fourth one, and this time the gap was just about six months! Pretty unbelievable, right?" I was not the one to give up; I smirked secretly.

"Wow! That is something. Now, listen. You will be thrilled to know that today…"

"I know! It is as if some people treat marriage like a game. It is as if they want to keep playing it repeatedly until they win. I can never understand how they manage to do it." I went on, ignoring you completely. I could see that you were now on the edge of your seat, and your smile had faded into a straight line.

"Anya, I have been trying to tell you something since the last half an hour. Will you for once stop blabbering and let me speak?" you said agitatedly.

Just then, the waiter approached, a sharply dressed short guy with a Charlie Chaplin moustache, stopping a step away from the table, sensing that you were about to lose your patience. You were about to be exasperated once again, but then you noticed him carrying not a pizza, but a cake.

"Congratulations, sir!" he said meekly, and placed the cake on the table, lit the candle and left just as quietly as he had appeared.

Surprise swept across your face and rested as a gleam in your eyes. You were speechless. "You, smartass!" you muttered as you came over to my side and enveloped me in a tight hug. At last, I got my reward for all the drama.

"*Now* you may tell me all about it," I told you, as I snuggled closer into your arms.

"Alright. So, as you guessed, I got the offer. What you would never have guessed is how I negotiated and upped the offer."

"Really now! How much raise did you manage?" I was very curious now. I had always trusted you to excel in your career (with your premiere-league MBA, you had managed a fair kick-start for yourself already), and this was just the beginning of a long and shining road ahead.

"Well, they were not keen on raising the package directly. But the brand has been growing across the Asia Pacific; they have been recruiting in several countries. And so, I negotiated on the location. I insisted that I want to be on the fast-paced trajectory. I suppose they liked my confidence and the go-getter attitude. So, guess what? Within an hour, the HR arranged for a call with their Singapore headquarters, and I was interviewed for the branding role in Singapore. And just as I was leaving office to meet you, I received the email confirming my appointment. So, my dear Anya, you are speaking to the new Brand Executive – Gainz Global Ltd., Singapore!"

You were barely able to control your excitement. Unfortunately, I was unable to come to terms with what I had just heard you say.

"So, *you* asked to move to Singapore?" I asked meekly, as if not saying it aloud would somehow stop it from happening.

"Yesss! And they agreed! Isn't that great news?"

Now, it was my turn to be speechless. I did not wish to dampen your excitement, but the news was so shocking I ended up speaking my mind before I could check my words.

"It is a great opportunity for *you*, not so much for me. You could have at least discussed with me once before making such a huge decision."

"I don't understand. Aren't you happy I got the offer? I mean, two minutes ago, you were ordering a cake, and now you are acting so cold. What's the matter?"

"The matter is that I didn't expect you to be moving to Singapore at this stage of our relationship. Here I was hoping that you would take the initiative to take things forward, plan on meeting my parents after your new job and think of being settled. Instead you go off in the opposite direction and take up a job in Singapore!"

"Yes, obviously, because it is a great opportunity. And you are acting as if I did not think about you at all. Rather, I was thinking long term for the both of us, not myself alone. Silly Anya! Did you think I will move there alone? If you did, then let me ask you to please start looking for a shift for yourself as well. I know it will take some time, but I am sure we can manage until then. Our love is strong enough to endure long distance for a while. After all, it is great for our future. What do you say?"

I felt ashamed at having misunderstood you.

"I do not have much time, Aarav. My parents probably won't wait for so long. They have already started talking about getting me married. If I don't tell them about you now, they will go and find some suitable guy for me on their own. I don't want to complicate things unnecessarily."

"Wait, you are the one complicating the matter here. If meeting your parents is a concern, let's do that tomorrow," you said it with such calmness that my worries disappeared in a moment.

"Really? You would do that?"

"Of course, sweetheart. Now let's have this cake, I can't resist it any longer."

I was so relieved and happy that you had agreed to meet my parents that I did not bother you with any other questions that evening.

The next day was a Saturday, so I was home with my parents. As with all recent weekends, they broached the topic of my marriage. One of my dad's friends who believed I would be a suitable match for his son had approached them.

"*Beta*, there was something I needed to discuss with you," my dad began what I had now understood was his standard opening line to discuss a prospective groom. After averting the topic for more than three months, I had now learned all the tactics Indian parents use to get their kids to consider settling down. I had no issues with settling down, but I wanted you to be on the same page as me when I spoke about you to my parents. Now that we were aligned on this point, I took my opportunity to tell my dad about you.

"Actually Dad, there's something I myself wanted to discuss with you," I told him. Smart that he is, my dad understood what I was referring to. This was the crucial moment – it could go in either direction from here – either he would be happy that I was finally showing interest in the prospect of settling down, or he could get furious like many other Indian parents at the thought of his daughter dating a guy and wanting to have the oh-so-tabooed 'love marriage'.

"Tell me about him," he said with a gentle smile that put me at ease instantly. He was probably cooler than I gave him credit for.

"His name is Aarav – Aarav Mehra. We met at the All India Marketers' Conference party, two years ago. He is from a nice Punjabi family in New Delhi. Just like me, he has also done his MBA after BTech, and he works with a boutique consulting firm right now, but will be joining Gainz Global Ltd. very soon," I told him about you, mostly factual information, intentionally keeping out the Singapore bit, should things go South before even beginning. "If you want, I can call him over and you can meet him."

And so, you joined us for dinner that evening. As agreed in our detailed discussion the previous day, you arrived on time, dressed in neat formals and greeted my parents by joining your hands in a *namaste*. Good start, I remember thinking when I noticed my mom look at dad approvingly. The evening was going surprisingly well. You and Dad seemed to have broken the ice fairly easily and were chatting away comfortably.

"So, Aarav, tell me about your family. How many of you, what do they do, do they know about you and Anya, how did they react etc... You know – the whole shebang," my dad asked you, as if chatting away casually with an old friend.

"Of course, uncle. My dad was with the merchant navy. He passed away five years ago. Since then, it was mom, my brother and me. My brother is in Canada, and he was married three years ago. In fact, my sister-in-law and he recently had a baby. And so, Mom has been staying there to help them settle in. She will be back in a few months. As for letting her know about Anya and me, she does know about Anya, in the sense that she is my friend and I suppose she has a hint that there might be something more."

A look of slight skepticism appeared over Dad's face when he realized your mom was not aware about us. This was where things got tricky.

"A hint. I see. I am assuming she will be open to accepting Anya into the family?"

"I don't see why not. I just don't want to rush things. Firstly, she is not in the country, and secondly, with me moving out soon, it makes more sense to wait until things settle down."

Oops, here it comes, I thought.

"You moving out meaning?" Dad's brow was in a furrow now.

"To Singapore, of course. I mentioned earlier about the job offer with Gainz Global Ltd.?"

"Yeah, but I didn't know it was in Singapore. When do you have to join?"

"As soon as the visa is processed."

"So how do you plan on taking things forward then if you won't be here?" Dad was in the typical father-of-the-bride mode now.

"I suppose for starters…" You got into talking business, adjusting your spectacles as you spoke, "Anya can also find a job there and then once we have our careers sorted, we can plan things ahead."

My dad did not say anything immediately. When he did, he said matter-of-factly, "I would need to speak with your mother, if we can proceed to make things formal," he smiled finally, satisfied with your sincerity.

I was so relieved to see the upward curve of my dad's lips, I went and hugged him tight, thanking him again and again. You were elated too, and even your confidence could not betray the relief in your eyes.

I thanked my stars for being so kind to have blessed us with such a smooth progression. However, I had not guessed I was being a little hasty in this, as fate seemed to have other plans for us…

About two days after meeting my dad, you called me at around midnight. I assumed you were trying to be romantic, but I only sensed worry in your voice.

"Anya, my brother just called me. My mom has taken ill, and I will need to rush to Toronto immediately. I know I promised your dad to have him speak to her, but it will take a while before I can arrange that."

"Please, Aarav. You do not need to worry about Dad at such a time. I will handle that. You please take care of your mom. When are you leaving?"

"I just booked the flight for early morning tomorrow. You please take care of yourself. I will be in touch soon."

The soon turned out a week later. You texted me to let me

know your mom had been detected with breast cancer and was undergoing intense treatments for the same. You added that you would be staying there a little longer, given your brother's baby was too young and he needed your support with your mom's treatment. I was supremely worried about your mom and knew you were under intense pressure, but I could not help missing you terribly.

A week turned to a month, and a month turned into three. Your mom's situation seemed to be improving, albeit very slowly. It was likely to take several more months for her to fully recover. As a result, you had requested Gainz Global to place you with their Toronto office instead of Singapore. Your request was accepted as an exception, and though the process took long, you seemed to have finally settled in.

This change was a huge dampener for our relationship, which had already taken a huge hit since your move – all with the different time zones, your stress about your mom's health and the distance itself. Now, with you taking up a job there, things had only gone further South. Up until now I had been defending your case confidently to my dad. However, of late, even he had started to get jittery. I was unsure how he would take this news of you moving your base to a different continent altogether.

At last, we agreed to let him know of the change in plans together by setting up a Skype call. I got him on the video chat that night, when you explained the entire scenario to him in detail.

At first, he was empathic about your situation. He liked the fact that you had stepped up to help out with matters at home. However, as father of the girl, he was restless to get some clarity from you as well.

"Young man, I appreciate that you are taking care of your mother so well. However, given that it has been more than a few months since our last chat, I want to know your plan on marrying my daughter. Tell me clearly, please."

I could see my dad was holding back his anxiety, and I was praying for you to come up with a good response.

"Of course, I want to marry your daughter, uncle. I just can't say how soon that will be. I am myself going through a major change, and I don't think it will be a good idea to add the burden of marriage at this point."

The word 'burden' kept looming in my head. Was I really hearing you call marriage to me a burden?

"I see how you consider marriage a burden." Dad picked up on the word, too. "Do you plan on at least getting engaged anytime soon?" his stance was very tensed now. I started to get very nervous as well, but I was sure of our love, and that you would stand up for it no matter what it took.

"Engagement or marriage, what's the difference? Honestly, uncle, I am not saying I won't marry Anya. I just cannot commit a date at this point in time."

Your tone was very firm now, which meant you had already made up your mind.

"So, you mean you can take six months or a year or two years or even eternity to commit."

"I am sorry, uncle. But that is how the situation is. Mom is going to need a much longer treatment than we had initially anticipated, and in such a situation, I do not want to bring in anything new into the picture. I hope you understand."

"Hmmm." Dad said, before turning to me and continuing, "Anya, I need to go and get your mother's medicines. I will see you later," and he walked off with that.

I could not blame my dad for his behavior. He was not one to be unreasonably pushy in such matters, but he definitely did not like the uncertainty. For a change, I could see he had a point. Not that I could blame you for the situation either. But here I was, pushing his patience to its limits, and I was not feeling good about leaving him hanging like that.

The next day, Dad and I were watching our daily news, when I noticed Mom giving him the look. Immediately after, he casually broached the topic.

"So, what have you thought about the matter? How long are you going to wait for him?" he asked, switching to an English news channel after hearing the anchor on Hindi news yelling out a melodramatic headline.

"Huh? Oh, well…" I was caught so off guard; I did not have an answer. I wanted to tell him I could wait an eternity for you, but of course, he would have shut me up for my silliness.

"Mohan uncle was talking about his nephew the other day at the wedding. He is with Microsoft in Bangalore and seems to be doing quite well for himself, Mom pitched in this time. "I saw his picture on WhatsApp. Looks fine. Good height, complexion…"

"Mom, please! Aarav is in real trouble right now. The least we can do is give him some time," I retorted.

"Yes, yes. I am not saying his intents are wrong. But *beta*, you need to understand that one needs to be practical at times. We have never stopped you from pursuing anything you wanted. When you wanted to move to a different city for your graduation, we were in fact proud that you were learning to be independent. When you brought the boy home, I was pleased with your choice and happy you had picked a sensible chap. However, as your parents, we worry about your future. And future does not wait for everything to be perfect. Take his own case. When the time came for him to take a bold step for his family, he took it. Now, don't get me wrong, there is nothing wrong in what he did. But now? Things are better now, and he needs to take another bold step for you this time. I don't see him even considering that right now."

"You are getting him wrong! He will take the step. We need to wait…" I was desperate now, "He will be back soon," I pleaded.

"Of course, the choice is yours. We can only guide you. But if you ask my opinion, it is time to move on. Think about it."

Dad's phone rang just then, and he got up to go to his room, pressing my shoulder comfortingly before he left. Mom followed him too.

I was on the brink of a breakdown that day. I stayed awake the whole night. We had just had a long chat and had argued inconclusively. You were so firm about not making things formal that I felt humiliated about begging you to reconsider your decision – all I wanted was for you to take up the discussion with your mother. I accused you of not taking our relationship seriously; you accused me back of not caring about your dilemma. I argued that things were starting to look better, and you argued back that your mom's treatment still had a long way to go and in turn accused me of being unnecessarily hasty. I shot back that we needed to show some haste given we were twenty-six and not twenty anymore, and you shot back by calling me desperate. That was it. Deny as we might, we both knew our end was inevitable.

The next couple of weeks we tried to make up for our harshness, but neither of us had an answer to help resolve the matter. We tried to work on several options, including long distance, but our hearts were simply not into it anymore. And so, three months later, after having tried to our best to survive the strain, we said our final goodbyes and parted ways.

I won't say I stopped loving you. No, I don't think that is

humanly possible for me. I wept many a nights after our breakup, trying to shun away your face that kept haunting my dreams, to forget the memories we had carved together, to not let my heart stagnate in the hope of you coming back someday. When the tears dried up, I had pushed you into a corner of my heart that I never wanted to access again; because even the memory of you brought such immense pain, that it had the potential to rip through my heart and burn through me like a wild fire.

Only a couple of years later, did I eventually learn to deal with life. Gradually, I started to bring forth my pragmatic side once again and dared to look at the world through a fresh set of eyes – ones that did not keep searching for you. Despite my fresh perspective, I knew I was rendered permanently incapable of loving another soul in this lifetime the way I had loved you. So, when the time came to put on a ring of another man's name, I chose one who promised companionship and compatibility over love. That is how I ended up with my husband.

PROMISES

Dearest Aarav,

I was still lost in my thoughts when I got pulled back to reality by the knock on the bathroom door. My husband needed to shower as well, and I needed to get myself together and get to work. Quickly, I dressed up and got myself ready to leave. Involuntarily, I gave one more look at my attire before leaving and added an extra dab of gloss to my lips. I couldn't help but smile to myself recalling the bliss from the previous night. No, parting was not an option this time. We were going to figure it out…

I had never been one to worry about performance at work. Excelling in a job came naturally to me. Part of this was because I had chosen a field of my interest as my profession. After having spent over a decade in planning strategies for leading brands, one could also say I was beginning to establish a name for myself in the industry.

Yet, no other assignment in the past had ever had me so excited as to make me look forward to a Monday. Work was to be another excuse to see you. It had been just two days since we had last met, and yet, my heart was behaving like a teenager who had just experienced her first crush. To think of it, perhaps that is all that you could have been – a passing phase – only, we had taken things a tad bit far to call it just that anymore.

So, for a change, I accepted things for what they were, and got dressed for our next meeting, an official one this time.

We met at your office that day. Both of us had our teams accompanying us for the discussion. Your team member, Anuj, the young rookie, took up the round of introductions and started the presentation. I was surprised despite myself at how we were able to mask our emotions and camouflage into the formal environment of business, the stereotypical 'client-agency' relationship. You were just as I had imagined you to be at work – sharp in your understanding and crisp in your commands. I had a feeling you must have left many of your subordinates in awe with your style of working (and otherwise). No wonder you are where you are today, heading the portfolio of the country's leading ready-to-cook food brands in a multinational conglomerate at a young age of thirty-six.

As for myself, I must admit I enjoyed the thrill of being in the advertising world – the joy of seeing the audience identify the products by the associations, taglines and jingles we presented to them; to see the brands grow from being nascent entrants in the market to an indispensable part of its loyal consumers' lives. Having spent a good part of the decade in my current firm, I was now part of the senior team leading key accounts, such as yours, junior only to the director and VP of the firm.

I was enjoying this meeting quite a bit. I am sure you are aware that I am referring to the sharp questions you kept shooting at me, completely ignoring those around us. I could see you enjoyed pulling us up on every small detail, no matter how minute its impact was to be to the actual project. Well mister, I wasn't where I was by sheer chance, so we had all your queries anticipated beforehand, with answers handy for each of them. So, on and off we went with the rapid-fire line of questions and solutions and challenges and workarounds.

Anyways, we spent half a day in that meeting after which the teams joined for a project kick-off lunch. I saw you make a random excuse to Anuj to ensure you got a seat next to mine. The young chap, eager to impress, obliged happily by offering to switch his own seat with me. And just like that, we were able to pick up from where we had left off. You started with a compliment this time, praising my skills. I returned the gesture and you made some silly joke about it, which for the life of me I cannot remember as I was so distracted by that dimpled smile of yours. I wonder if my team noticed my blush. If they did, they surely did not comment, but I can say one thing – you did leave the young girls in my team infatuated with your charm. I know from the discussion we had on our way back to office from there – your spell had seemed to broaden its audience. I don't quite know their sources, but they seemed to know all about you already – single, hot guy with a 3-bedroom flat in Bandra! I even saw Tania – one of the girls from my team, or rather one of your latest fan club members – check out your social profile. Well, nothing new for me there – I had already seen it multiple times since Sunday and knew your timeline by heart now. On second thoughts, I can't believe I just admitted this! Even as I write this, I am feeling immature. Perhaps that is what love does to all – takes away the sanity from maturity and leaves behind immature innocence.

Fortunately, I wasn't the only one being silly here. I saw your attempts supersede mine when you reached out through mails and texts messages for the smallest of reasons. From that point on, all barriers to communication were broken. I found you checking in on me several times through the day, sometimes through reasons pertaining to work, sometimes through just a casual hello. Soon enough we would be treading on the path of silliness of teenage romance, sharing clichés of 'miss you' texts to each other at intervals of a mere couple of hours!

A week or so passed this way and our virtual rendezvous continued. I was finding my smile return. The sprint in my step was a telltale sign evident to all. A very good friend of mine from office, Ritu, also asked me if I was on a special diet that was giving me the glow. I blatantly lied to her that it was the fruits – how they detoxified the body and the soul. Little did she know how dark my soul had turned since I had bumped into you.

We were to meet that Friday, after office, and although we had already met twice that week over official meetings, I was impatient for the day to pass so I could be with you again, in an informal setting – just the two of us, without any agenda to discuss or issues to resolve. I had planned the work to avoid last minute delays. I had even messaged my husband that I was likely to be late at work, so he need not wait up for dinner. And I made sure I retouched my make-up before leaving office (yes, I had started using makeup. You see how I was starting to change for you?).

A pang of nervousness started creeping up inside me just as I was entering the restaurant's parking lot. A second date would imply that things were getting serious. No longer was it just a fling that happened in the heat of the moment. This one was to be a conscious step into involving ourselves into a full-blown affair. The decision was my own, not forced on by anyone, not impulsive, and not momentary. This was to be a thought-through, rational call taken by an adult woman well aware of the consequences of her decision on her marriage. Was I ready to risk it? Was it even worth the risk? And most importantly, was it even real? Surely it couldn't be. Like a silly teenager, I was letting myself fall for this make-believe fairytale of perfect romance.

Still lost in this potpourri of indecisive thoughts, I entered the restaurant full of self-doubt. I was on the verge of convincing myself to end whatever this was that was going on between us. Then, I saw you waiting for me at the window-side table. You were nervously running your fingers through your hair, glancing at your watch and fidgeting in your seat. I took these as signs that you were just as skeptical about the entire thing as I was, and this made me realize that you were also as vested in this as me, that I was not a passing girlfriend for you. I am not sure why, but it made me feel better, somewhat less guilty about seeing a man outside my marriage. Or perhaps that is what I used as an excuse to allow myself to be carried away once again.

Despite my newfound excuse, my face must have shown traces of the turmoil in my head, for the moment I entered you asked me if something was bothering me. I obviously denied it, but you refused to give up. Still unsure if I wanted to have this discussion with you now, I muttered a barely audible 'Everything'. Surprisingly you heard it, as well as everything else that was yet unsaid, for you looked visibly taken aback. Those eyes that were gleaming just two seconds ago were now dry of all joy. Your mouth twitched into a straight, thin line, and your body fell back into the seat.

"I don't know why, but I was half expecting this. It was, after all, too good to be true," you said, reading my mind. Only, hearing you say this shattered me in a way I had not imagined. Your words left me speechless, but my soul was screaming from within. The thought of not having you in my life anymore seemed real now in this moment, and it jolted me from within, upset me, scared me! I had not expected to feel so strongly about losing you.

Yet, there I was, too afraid to let you go, too afraid to step out of infidelity while I still had the chance.

Therefore, instead of grabbing the chance to call it quits before it was too late, I sprang into your arms and kissed you like never before, asking you to never let me go.

Gentle as a dove, you then lifted my face, looked into my eyes and promised, "I will always be with you."

"Is that even possible?" I asked you, still holding you tight, scared I might lose you if I let go.

You just smiled after that, kissed my forehead and hid me in your arms. Even if you had not said anything after that, I would have known what our being together meant to you. Yet, your words cushioned me in a cozy blanket of warmth that my heart had been craving since the last eight years.

You said, "Anya, if you are wondering what we are doing here, given that you are married, then please know this – I do not care about these social tags that people wear around their necks for life. You and I both know very well that the bond we share is special, beyond any of these superficial, social obligations. I do not care that you are married, but I do know that you are not in a fulfilling marriage; else, you would not have been here. And I cannot see you waste any moment of your life being less than happy. And if I may, I have taken it upon myself to make sure you stay above the line that distinguishes a happy life from mere existence at all times. Moreover, as long as you are with me, I can assure you that I will be in the happy-life zone as well. That is all I want from you, from us."

I could only smile after hearing you say this. However, it still did not help put my guilt at ease. "But surely we can't be like this forever? It is still wrong," I muttered to you.

"We will cross that bridge when we come to it. For now, I can only ask you for your present."

With those words, I realized I did not care about 'always'. All that mattered was that present, the present with you. That I was thankful to have just found you. And for such moments with you, I could trade the world. No, the world did not matter either. For such moments with you, I could trade eternities. Yet, in the end, eternities would not matter; these moments would, as a lifetime was lived in every moment I spent with you.

Bliss

Dearest Aarav,

Time flew by. Six weeks had passed since our reunion and we had met sixteen times — not that I intended to keep a count.

As our dates got more and more frequent and intimate, we realized we needed to have some time to ourselves away from the prying world. So, we planned our first getaway.

I cannot quite recall how we arrived at the decision. I think it was because meeting in the city was too stressful, time bound. Planning fake meetings to justify my late arrivals to my husband, rushing back home to meet family commitments (or more likely the routine of duties), the constant uneasiness of being in a space that was not rightfully 'ours' – I guess it was getting too much. We needed some time off from all the running around, and space where we could be ourselves. While we did spend a fair bit of time at your place, the sense of 'cheating' was quite overwhelming in that room – your room! Perhaps that was why I happened to mention it casually to you the other day. Little did I know that you would actually take it seriously. In fact, you were almost too excited about it. No wonder you sold off the idea to me so convincingly, in your standard, charming style – do you remember that? Over a cup of coffee in your balcony, while we were watching the sunset, you said you wanted to take me to a place where we could witness this beauty without any worry on our minds. Somewhere away from the rush — in a space where we could be just 'us' — carefree, thought-free. How could a mortal being like me have resisted such a temptation from a demi-god such as you!

Remember how meticulously we planned for it? Right from deciding the location to figuring out the perfect excuse to tell my husband (did you notice how I was slowly getting over my guilt of betraying him?) to finalizing the hotel! Everything had to be special, as if we were going on a vacation the first time, having forgotten the many such escapades from years ago!

Anyhow, we decided to go on a weekday to avoid suspicion. It had to be masked as an official trip, of course. So, I made up a fake conference as a cover up to tell my husband. As usual, I had my 'excuse' speech prepared and rehearsed. And as usual, he showed little interest in the entire thing – there was neither worry nor excitement in his reaction. His indifference always shocked me, although I should have gotten used to it by now.

We met directly at the airport that morning for our 7 am flight to Goa. Only after boarding the flight did it actually sink in that we were indeed off!

Like a thorough gentleman, you had pre-booked our pickup that took us to Grand Hyatt – you liked to travel in style, I gathered. Oh, how beautiful those two days were – so very different from all the times before when I had visited Goa, yet most special. The narrow, entwining roads under the canopy of lush green trees seemed more charming this time. The church bells rang a sweeter melody this time. The smell of the sea was balmier this time. And the wind in my hair had draped me in romance this time – one that adorned me from head to toe in your love.

The view from our room was so beautiful, I wanted to spend the entire day staring out of it at the sea that lay just a few meters affront. But of course, the bed suited us more, and kept us occupied most of the time.

We revelled in the barefoot walk at the hotel's private beach of the Bambolim bay in the morning, followed by a long bath in the tub together, and then driving up North to watch the sunset while smoking the hookah at the shacks of Baga, and finally the candle lit dinner by the poolside of the hotel. It was a perfect day.

"So much has changed," I had said then, on our second night there while crossing my feet over each in the lazy chair overlooking the pool, sipping Mai Tai, and you had instead replied, "Nothing has changed at all."

Everything was so perfectly charming, or perhaps your charm made everything more beautiful. My favourite part was our morning cup of coffee and the scrumptious breakfast we lazily gulped lying on our bed. That time made me conscious of the long path we had treaded in our journey to this point.

There was a time, when we were young and adventurous, naïve and reckless. But those days had its own charm. We were still strugglers in our respective careers, so our fine-dine nights were limited to special occasions. Gifts were mostly handcrafted cards, collages or videos. And when we wanted a romantic evening, Carter Road at Bandra was our calling. Oh well, how can I speak of Carter Road and not mention your *jugaad* to fix us a drink by the sea? You do recall what *jugaad* I am referring to, don't you?

✳ ✳ ✳

It was a perfect evening – not too cold, not too humid. As part of our Friday routine, we had met up at Bandra to spend the evening together. We headed to Carter Road and found a spot for ourselves on the pavement, overlooking the sea. We were just beginning to get cozy, keeping an eye out for the cops while stealing a few kisses. It was a beautiful day – you beside me, I in your arms, the sea in front of us. If only we could share a drink…

"Why not!" you had exclaimed at my suggestion instantly.

"But how?" I asked, as it was against the law to drink on the streets.

"I have just the right solution. Come, let's go," you said, getting off and grabbing me.

"But I want to drink here, facing the sea!" I protested as you took me away from my favourite view.

"Yes, yes. We will come back, don't worry."

You called for an auto rickshaw then.

"*Bhaiya*, we need to go to this place near Hill Road, have five-minutes of work there, and then we will come back here. Can you take us?"

We hopped in, you directed the driver to turn right, and then left and then again, some more turns until we reached some narrow alleys of Bandra's residential area. There, you found a winery. You asked me to wait in the auto rickshaw, while you got down to make your purchase.

When you got back, you had two bags in your hand. One had two bottles of Sprite.

"Drink it up," you told me.

I had no idea where you were going with this, but we shared that bottle of Sprite and near-emptied it within a couple of minutes. This is where it got interesting – you then pulled out the other bag. It had two miniature vodka bottles. You opened the first one and transferred the contents into this empty Sprite bottle. I watched in awe as you did all this in a moving auto rickshaw, without spilling so much as a drop. Next, out came the other Sprite bottle, and about three-fourth of it was emptied into the first Sprite bottle, which now already had vodka. *Now* I figured what you had just done. You repeated the process with the other bottle, and well, well, well, we had our drinks ready, disguised in bottles of aerated drinks! Come cops; catch us if you can!

What fun that day was! That trick of yours became our standard fix for all the times we went to the seaside after that day.

Just as this was our little moment. Looking at your face the first thing in the morning was the most special memory that I took away from the trip. I can't tell you how I wished to have that privilege every day, and how I convinced myself to not let my mind wander away into that complicated land. I had to keep reminding myself that one cannot have everything in one lifetime, and I had already received more than my share of happiness when I found you.

Bringing myself back to the present, I remember thinking to myself how blissful even that present was in its own way. Do you recall arguing about Ayn Rand's philosophy of objectivism? Your 'oh-so-revolutionary' self, surfaced when I questioned you on the extremism of her belief system upon seeing you read *The Anthem*. It was a fun duel, wasn't it – to talk about how important it was to sometimes put our own happiness before others. For once, I was pleasantly surprised to see you think so pragmatically and clearly, of the impact of our actions in the long run. I was also proud of my stance in seeing the broader picture in everyone's happiness. I think this was the first time we both sported bold views reflecting our core natures, for in all aspects, I indeed was the more social one, whereas you were more driven by your personal agendas. Although it was a fun discussion and a pleasant change to talk about things we believed in, to talk about our principals, life, dreams, and goals, without constantly thinking simply about our future and ourselves together; little did I know then that this contrast in our natures would one day bring us to the point where we are today…

✳ ✳ ✳

Like all happy times, the three days seemed to have gone by in the blink of an eye. In a way, the getaway brought us closer and roused our want of each other so much that we couldn't wait to see each other at every opportunity thereafter. We started coming up with smart as well as silly excuses to set up out-of-office meetings. Sometimes, it was a contract extension discussion, sometimes a small detail needed to be discussed in person; sometimes it was a friend's birthday and sometimes a shopping trip.

With such manoeuvres, it was quite inevitable and just a matter of time before we were caught in public.

Do you remember that day when we were lunching at the *Pizza by the Bay* and a friend of my husband's – Diya – ran into us? I was most skeptical of her getting suspicious – for she had always been that way, especially given that she was my husband's ex. I had had my doubts as to whether she had ever really gotten over him! I wondered if she would notice that we were sharing our drink – something quite trivial I know, but with Diya around, I could never be too sure.

She greeted me with her pretentiously cheerful smile, her sling-bag swooshing at her hips as she waved and walked over in her stilettoes. I noticed her giving you a look from head to toe as she went about the formalities, while running her hand through her straightened blonde hair.

"Well, hello there, Anya!" she exclaimed.

Unaccustomed to being caught, I fumbled during the course of simple introductions. Obviously, you had to be introduced as a client, but the hiccup must have been obvious, as Diya instantly gave us that suspicious glare from the corner of her eye.

"Honestly, I never imagined bumping into you here – isn't this place too far away from your office?" she continued, making her suspicions a little too obvious.

Even here, you salvaged the situation by interjecting, "Anya was too kind to come all the way for our convenience – my firm was hosting an event right across," you said, while coolly handing over your business card and diverting the topic to some business matter. I realized then how poor I was at disaster management!

Although we had a good laugh over the entire incident later, I was still jittery about the entire scene, particularly given Diya's history with my husband. As you know Aarav, at one point in time, my husband and Diya were dating. While my husband did not see a future with her, Diya had vested her emotions for the long haul. It took her some time to get over my husband and only after she got married was she able to re-establish the friendly terms with him. Therefore, despite being happily married herself, I had always sensed a tinge of jealousy from her whenever we had interacted in the past.

Little did we know then that my jitters were for a valid reason after all, as that, this seemingly harmless incident would one day very sneakily cause us a grave issue.

CONJECTURE

Dearest Yohan,

The best part of our relationship was that we were genuinely good friends, rather, the best of friends. And the downside of being best friends with your spouse is that they can sense your lies without you speaking them.

That is why it surprised me the most when you did not notice the change in my demeanour. Did you not see us growing apart? Did you not catch even one of the many the blatant lies I kept telling you? Did you not doubt my silly excuses for late nights and getaways even once? Did you really fail to notice anything at all, or did it just not matter to you anymore?

There was a time when you would guess my mood the moment I stepped into the house. That was the time when you cared about me and took genuine interest in my life. Surely, you remember how we would discuss our days in detail with each other over a late night drink in our balcony? How you took efforts to learn my taste in the dishes you cooked for me, and surprised me often with your specialty 'butter chicken', customized to my taste? You knew all of my colleagues and friends and had met up with most of them. You did not show your concern when I would be late from work, but you would always stay up when I had those miserable long-night assignments and put such an effort in making me unwind after such terribly hectic days. There never was a day when we slept off on a bad note, not even when we fought our worst fights.

And we were so good as a team. Perfectly in sync. Remember what your friends – Sushant and Ahana – used to say about us? That we were like Monica and Chandler, except that Chandler was actually funny. How much fun it used to be to hang out with them, to host those parties on weekends, to play the game of Catan that stretched into the wee hours of the morning and then laze around until afternoon on Saturdays, only to resume it again in the evening! Oh, and do you remember that New Year's Eve house party that we had thrown? We had invited all your friends over, with spouses, of course – a good twenty people we are talking about. Yet, everything went so smoothly. You prepared the invites, I sent out the reminders. You took care of the food; I managed the décor. You arranged the booze; I arranged the games. Oh, speaking of games…weren't we simply the best? We beat everyone at Pictionary with a perfect score. I doubt anyone has even managed a perfect score ever. We should have seriously registered a record in our names for it! And let me not even get started on the bluff card game. Not once did we let each other get away with our bluffs. How well we knew each other. How perfect we were as a team.

I miss those days. I miss my partner…I miss us. Especially, because we were good together. We were so good. What went so wrong then?

If I look back now, I feel the crux of our issues started about two years into the marriage. Until then, we had been okay. Yes, we had our share of arguments; we had our share of disagreements, but nothing we could not resolve. Yet, the change had been gradual. Over a period, as we had started to evolve into our older selves, particularly with the thirties setting in, we had started to drift apart as individuals.

For your part, I could see that you had started staying more and more involved in your work. I won't be unfair by saying you did not try to get any time off, but just that the role demanded so much out of you, you barely had anything else left to offer to anyone else, including me. You were gaining success, which was getting you recognition, which in turn motivated you to give more to your work and the cycle continued. Somewhere in the process, you lost zeal in anything else.

I used to love being with the Yohan that was sporty and up for any adventure – be it an impromptu getaway or an experiment in bed (have I ever mentioned I enjoyed our kinkiness?) I respected that you had varied interests in life – reading, cycling, cooking (something you had cultivated after we got married – thanks to my horrible skills in the kitchen). Now, you barely had time for any of the things you loved. Your work had consumed you entirely, so much, so that any interruption at any moment would make you snap. We moved into a bigger house, but along with that, the hole of emptiness in our marriage grew bigger as well.

At first, I tried to point it out to you, to make you understand how you were losing track of the things that mattered to you. Initially, you even took the feedback positively, albeit, without reflecting anything in your behavior. Gradually, though, even that stopped. You became outright rude when I tried to coax you into taking a break or calling it a night at 2 a.m., as you looked as if you desperately needed some rest. I remember one occasion when you had come back home exhausted but happy, as you had closed a big deal that evening. I suggested that now that you had finally closed a milestone, perhaps, we should head out somewhere to take a well-deserved break and celebrate your success. Moreover, we had not really gone out since our last anniversary – and that was over ten months ago! However, you made the suggestion seem so outrageous that I wondered if I had indeed committed some grave mistake I had not realized. Then you justified. Your excuse – this is the time for you to close more deals. It was as if you were intoxicated. And when one is intoxicated, it is best to not nudge one in a forced direction. With that, I stopped interfering in your life completely.

A few days later, though, you apologized for your behavior. You said you had lost your temper in the heat of the moment, you did not mean it, blah blah. I could see you were sorry for the way you had acted that day in particular, but not sorry for your behaviour in general. You did not see anything going awry. In fact, the icing on the cake was when you suggested that we should probably consider starting a family, as that would solve our problems. You said, and I remember this clearly, that once a baby comes, I will have something to focus on, and become less dependent on you. How crude it was of you to put it like that! I denied your proposition outright and claimed I did not need a baby to stop feeling dependent on you. But the suggestion did make me realize I was indeed becoming too dependent on you – something so contrary to how I had always been. That wake-up call got me to focus on myself, and my own career, with a renewed zest.

Coming back to your suggestion on family planning, I had assumed the matter had ended then. But a month or two later, you again came back with the ask of starting a family. This time you said it was time, as we had already been married for over two years, almost three, for that matter. Now, not that I did not want a child myself, in fact it was something I had myself always wanted from marriage all along. But I could clearly see that we were not ready for one as yet. Not only were we not spending enough time with each other to emotionally reach that stage, but we were also becoming bitter towards each other. More importantly, I did not see your attitude changing anytime soon, and I was clear about not being the sole caregiver to a baby. Therefore, my stance on the matter remained unchanged.

You see, Yohan, when I decided to marry you, I was looking for an anchor of stability that the love of my life had refused me. And although you provided me with ample stability, what our marriage lacked at that point in time was love, passion. And a loveless marriage cannot create a family.

However, the idea kept growing in your head. What was initially a suggestion grew into a request and transformed into a demand. Your obsession with wanting a baby grew to such an extent that it became the sole objective of your life with me. It did not matter that in the process I had to endure your ill behavior. Neither did it matter to you to ask about my happiness or my choice, or even try to understand why I was not ready to bear a child. So lost were you in your own wants that you forgot to consider mine.

This might seem like a small thing to you, but if the entire existence of a marriage lies on whether you can bear your spouse a child or not, then therein lies a serious problem for you as a person in this relationship. The relationship reduces to one wherein you transform from an individual into just a wife and a mother. You cease to be an individual. You cease to be you.

But the sad state of our relationship was not your fault alone. When I noticed the first cracks in our relationship, however minute they were, I started pushing you away. When I should have held you close and loved you more, I started to avoid you instead. In my immaturity, I expected you to come to me in wholeness – as much emotionally as physically – if you must come to me at all. The truth, however, was that I could have made you whole, if only I had let you in. But that sensibility had yet to find me, and so I went about pushing you away. I made lame excuses to avoid sex – sometimes a body ache, sometimes the wrong time of the month. I opined then that sex made no sense if you were so consumed by your other obligations as to want it as a mere necessity.

As it is with most humans, men in particular, physical and the emotional fulfillment go hand-in-hand. When I had taken away the physical from our relation, you took away the emotional. This was probably because you mistook my stance as a gimmick that I was I pulling to avoid any chance of conceiving. This angered you even more, and your frustration with me increased further. As your frustration increased, my aversion towards you increased as well. And thus, we had been pulled into the vicious circle of assumptions and its repercussions.

Yohan, looking back upon our downhill journey that day I recalled this one conversation that I had once with my friends in college. We were discussing relationships and fidelity. While all of us had in unison said infidelity was unacceptable, there was this one girl who had taken a more lenient stance and said that should her partner ever cheat on her, she would want to try and 'understand the underlying cause' for his slip and see if he was somewhere justified in his actions. The perspective had seemed so outrageous at the time. I remember arguing with her on how wrong she was to think so, how loyalty was the foundation of a successful relationship, how even a slip was like a crack in the mirror, which can never go away completely no matter how much you tried to fix it. But then she had said something, which I had failed to understand back then. Only now, when I am in a similar situation myself, am I able to comprehend it fully.

She had said that when two people fall in love and decide to be together, they use this love as the bond that ties them. At some point in time, if one of the two people involved goes astray, it means the bond was cut loose at that end. The question is what caused the tension to break this bond? She had said, in this sense, relationships were like that law of physics – a bond is only as strong as its weakest link. In case of marriage, the bond string comprises of several elements – love, friendship, trust, honesty, care, respect, attraction, possessiveness and so on. Friction in either of these elements can weaken the bond, and from then on, it is just a matter of time before it all falls apart! How unjust then it would be to assume infidelity to be the cause rather than the effect of breakage of this bond?

As I lay in bed that night, I tried to fathom which element of our bond of marriage had become loose to cause this rupture. Thoughts turned to doubts and doubts turned to guilt. Before I knew it, I had wasted away another night lying awake, yet miles away from finding any answers...

SCANDAL

Dearest Aarav,

People say you fight the most with the ones you love the most. Somehow, I never believed that. Aren't the most loved ones too precious to pick fights with, to hurt? And especially with someone you are so compatible with; shouldn't there be minimal avenues for disagreement? Well, that's what I had thought about us as well.

We were so alike, and so aligned on even the smallest of things, I never thought that an expectation gap could exist between us. It was as if we had telepathic powers – you could guess what was on my mind without me ever telling you, and of course, vice versa. When I was worried about something, you would sense it and be there with a warm cup of coffee and a snuggle to comfort and pacify me – before I had even spelled the "w" of worry. When you were thrilled about something at work, I would see it in your eyes before you announced it. More than anything, we could be each other's confidants on professional matters, and we were proud of the fact that we were so unbiased in our views.

Like the other day, I was so worked up about Sunendu Mishra – the Director of my firm, and my boss – bringing in another account manager to work alongside me on your company's campaign. While I had seen it as a personal attack on my capabilities, you pointed it out (rightly so) that I needed to get pragmatic about the fact that the project scope was getting too big to be handled by one team alone. On the other hand, when I had become lax in pushing for my promotion, you had forced me into being vocal about my ambition.

"You need to be unabashed in asking about what you deserve. After all, you only get what you ask for," you had said then, pushing me to be the best version of myself, as always.

At the same time, I acknowledged your drive for success and pushed you to achieve great heights in your own role as well – even if it meant significant time apart to allow you to travel to the many cities your company operated in. The upside – the sex that came afterwards.

Do you recall the week-long conference you had at Lavasa? All you kept talking about while you were there was how you wished I was there with you. Well, little did you know of the surprise that lay ahead…

Come the last day of your conference and you had a surprising call from the front-desk right before your checkout. Apparently, they had mixed up your bags with someone else's and had sent them up to the guest's room instead of packing it up in your car. Annoyed by the long time they were taking to resolve the matter; you took it upon yourself to visit the guest's room and sort it out yourself.

"Well mister, did you find what you came looking for?" I had said, opening the door to your surprised face.

It took you less than a minute to figure out the entire gimmick, to give me a notorious smile before grabbing me by the waist and planting a deep, passionate kiss, right there at the door.

"Oh! You bet I did," you said as you lifted me up and wrapped my legs around your waist and carried me right into the room, flopped me onto the bed and undid the buttons of my blouse. The week-long wait had been more than worthwhile.

"I missed you more than I anticipated," you said quietly, as we lay in bed afterwards.

"I know," I replied all-knowingly, before planting you another kiss. "I don't know how we will carry on with this façade for long."

You hushed me with a finger on my lip, and kissed my cheeks before whispering, "You do not need to worry about anything, sweetheart. Whatever it is, we will deal with it together."

You laid my heart at rest with your sweet nothings, and I remained oblivious to the fact that we had not explicitly discussed our relationship status, or our future for that matter. Yet somehow, I knew it was pointless to jump the gun and spend our precious time together discussing (and probably arguing) about the future, while the present seemed to fulfill our needs fairly well. Moreover, we were confident about finding a way out when the time came. Albeit, I did not realize the time would arrive so soon.

*****

Something odd happened that day. Maybe it had been going on since quite some time, and I had only noticed it that day. This was during one of our official meetings, when as always, I had stayed back post presentation to simply catch up (in the room) with you. I vividly remember not spending too long; it must have been barely five minutes, because I knew my team was waiting outside. However, as I stepped out into the lobby of your office building to join the rest of the team, I caught a glimpse of a smirk escape Krisha's (one of my junior team member) face. Almost at the same moment, I noticed my team's director, Sunendu Mishra, (who had joined us this time, given it was the quarterly meet) also turn his head away, as if trying to avoid meeting my eye.

I would probably not have given the incident much heed had it not been followed by another one at office later that evening. We had gathered for the quarterly revenue discussion, where we typically take stock of ongoing projects, pipeline and align our strategy for the coming months. Normally, it is the account leads, the directors and the vice president, who assemble for this quarterly meeting. The vice president presides by leading the discussion, taking updates from the directors for their respective product categories, and the directors in turn rely on us account leads to provide a thorough review of the clients we manage. The group is small, barely eight to ten of us. Yet, this core group essentially dictates the course of the company. Every word spoken here is taken seriously. So, you can imagine why I was disturbed when Sunendu made an innuendo about my relationship with you in that meeting.

"E&M Foods account is sorted," he said, adjusting his fat-rimmed glasses and looking up at me from above them, "It will only grow from here on. Anya here has figured exactly how to hit just the right notes with Aarav Mehra, their head of marketing, the guy who holds the budgets." And once again, he smiled at me, or rather smirked at me. I felt blood rush to my cheeks, which I'm sure must have turned red as I noticed at least two others look down and smile.

"That's good to know, Anya," inferred my VP, Animesh Srivastava, "Now that this is in the bag, I am putting in at least one big one in your pipeline for the quarter, I hope that is fine," he said directly to me this time. I had always considered Animesh to be a thorough professional in matters of work, never half expecting him to react the way he did. Which is why I was so flustered by now that I could have torn apart both – his and Sunendu's faces. Afraid of blurting out brash words, I pretended to be engrossed in my laptop, but not before a glaring look at Sunendu.

The incident disturbed me so much, I was unable to get any critical work done the rest of the day. Clearly, gossip about us was making its rounds in office, and as the case always is, the subject was the last one to know about it. Shyna was the one to bring the news to me.

"Anya, I don't want to sound gossipy, but I hope you know you are becoming the talk of the town about your 'scene' with the E&M guy," she said one day, taking me to the side of the cafeteria. I was taken by such surprise, that I instinctively denied it – even though Shyna was the one friend I could have confided to. I just hoped that she would be able to put a stop to the grapevine.

Yet, later I was so upset that I was unable to think clearly, even to decide my course of action. Should I approach the HR department and raise a formal complaint against Sunendu? But what hard evidence did I have to prove that Sunendu in fact made the comment in a demeaning way? Animesh will obviously support him, as would the others, to save their own back. Maybe I should have a one-on-one conversation with him myself. But that will shut *him* up, not everybody else. God knows how far the rumour had already spread! Not to mention, bringing this up with Sunendu, even if informally, would mean inciting him against me. In such cases, there is always undue backlash on the one lower in the food chain. Moreover, I did not trust my temper should a situation of confrontation arise.

Finally, unsure of what to do, I decided to seek your opinion. You would definitely know what needed to be done. I rang you up and fixed a meeting with you for evening. Next, I called my husband to inform him of some last-minute project deliverable (I was surprised at how smooth I was becoming at making excuses. Unfortunately, I was also surprised at my husband's indifference every time. I mean, all things apart, the least he could have done was check on how late I would be or if I had company back home or about dinner or anything else! Just a little concern, for a change!).

Anyways, I met you that evening at Starbucks. I reached there before time, only to receive your text saying you were running late. I was supremely fidgety for the entire forty-five minutes that I waited for you. I was on my third cappuccino when I saw you enter the café. I hugged you as soon as you reached the table. Obviously, you sensed something was off and set off to enquire immediately. Over a glass of creamy frappe, I described the entire event to you.

"There it is. I feel like running away and hiding somewhere!" I summarized and waited for your magic solution.

To my utter surprise, you barely flinched! If anything, you were set to treat the entire episode very lightly.

"Is *that* what you were so upset about?" you asked casually.

"Yes, don't you see how it is just the start of the rumour-mill? It is only a matter of time before it reaches my husband. And worst of all, it is in my face, in my workplace! I will need to face it every single day. I have no idea what to do," I exclaimed, still not sure how you could take it so lightly.

"Relax; it's not such a big deal. It's just some new gossip for the office guys, and like all gossip, this one will go away too. You just chill," you assured, still quite composed.

"But aren't you worried?"

What you said next was probably something I had never expected. All along, I had thought you genuinely cared for me. However, what you said next shocked me.

"Hey, look. Honestly, I think you are missing the point here. If the VP, what's his name – Animesh – has asked you to extract a deal by taking advantage of your relationship with me, I think it is a disguised opportunity for you."

"What do you mean?"

"I mean that in any case you guys were going to get the project, regardless of you or me. So why not just keep mum and take the credit for the win?"

"No! I can't do that. And you are missing the point here. I don't want people at my workplace to be gossiping about me. I can't meet their eye, it is too awkward," I said, not quite understanding how you managed to see the 'business angle' in every matter.

"Since when did you start caring about society, Anya? People will gossip today and forget tomorrow. You should not let such trivial matters bother you. Anyway, sometimes it is good to be pragmatic. Think of the long-term benefit in this case. You stand to gain more than lose." Your matter-of-fact side was back.

"Long term? You and your long-term perspective, Aarav! Your long-term plan is the reason why we are standing here today, in case you don't remember," I shot back, digging up the old grave.

You were momentarily shocked by my blunt retort. But giving up has never been your nature. And so, the duel went on.

"Oh, I do remember, Anya. At least my plans included the both of us, unlike your selfish, myopic vision that did not include anybody except yourself. And honestly, our so-called 'situation' here gave me the impression that these past years must have taught you a thing or two about recognizing what's important and be bold enough to go get it. Sadly, I was mistaken. You are still the narrow visioned girl from eight years ago, who will never have the courage to step up for herself, let alone use the situation to your advantage."

Now, it was my turn to be shell-shocked. I had no idea you were capable of making me feel so little in my own eyes. When had you become so business-like in your approach to matters of the heart? This was a side of you I had never seen before. Had the years apart changed you so much? Had I been too blind to see the new, changed Aarav? Unable to hold back my anger, I stood up and left, teary-eyed.

Your caustic words stayed with me for a long time afterwards. As a result, I ended up avoiding you. When I did not take your calls a few times, you texted me mentioning you were sorry for being so harsh. While I replied with an okay, I could not get the incident out of my head. Incidentally, you had a product launch coming up, so you had to be out of city for a couple of weeks, so you sent messaged me a "love you" text instead. I texted you with a "thanks", but decided it was for the best that you were going to be away for a while; it would give me a few days to wrap my head around what was going on, and how I wanted to deal with things. But of course, life had a different plan – to spin my head, and life…

Proposition

Dearest Yohan,

"I missed you!" you exclaimed and hugged me the moment I entered the house that day. I hugged you back, only to realize the spark between us that was breathing its last breaths when I had met you, had now completely vanished. You must have sensed the awkwardness, so you asked me if everything was okay. I lied, of course, that I had a headache due to all the odd hour travelling (well, not entirely a lie if you look at it). To my surprise, you handed me a glass of water, led me to the bedroom and offered me a head massage. That night, we had sex after over two months.

You know Yohan; there is this strange thing about marriage. Even when all the love is gone, one can still manage to be intimate with one's spouse. I figured that day that I was capable of lying to you, not just to your face, but I could pull it off fairly well in bed too. It was as if I was developing a sort of a mask – I put it on and I'm the ideal wife, I pull it off and I can bare my soul and be the woman *he* desired. Which of these two was my actual face? Or was there something more beneath all these layers I was putting on?

The realization made me sick in the stomach. What was I becoming? As an outsider, I hated myself for the dual faced person that I was. It was that turning point in life, when the principles I had endured and resolved during my early adulthood were turning grey, and I knew there was more black than white in this grey.

I wonder what caused the transformation. Surely, it could not have been all *him*. Surely, this dark side had existed within me, like the opposing forces of the Yang in the Yin – with the Yin in me lying dormant, waiting for its time to mingle with the Yang and slowly turn everything dark.

Once again, as part of my bedside musing ritual, I pondered about how ignorant you could be about what was going on with me. Did you genuinely not suspect anything at all? We might not exactly have been soul mates, but surely, we were very good friends. And, good friends sense when something is wrong with the other person. By that logic, maybe you did know something was off and you intentionally chose not to react. On the other hand, why would you not react?

That's when it dawned on me that today wasn't an exception – the little changes had been showing in your behaviour in the last few days, I had been just too indifferent to notice. There wasn't anything major, really. Just little things here and there. Like the other day, I was late from my date night, and you obviously thought it was from work. So, you made me a drink so I could unwind. I can't believe you stayed up for me like old times, sat by my side and chatted about your work, asked me about my job and even talked about your plans on switching to another one with a better work-life balance so you could spend more time with me.

Now, I know how much you loved your work. Crazy as it might be in the investment banking field, you enjoyed the madness in the chaos. And you were good at it too – the best closer – as your best friend from work, Sushant – used to say about you. Therefore, when you talked about switching jobs, I knew something was not right.

This was new, and this was not you! There had to be something more than was meeting the eye. I thought of probing you about what was causing this change, but if you were doing it consciously, you clearly would not admit it. I thought perhaps I was overanalyzing, maybe my guilt was making me see things that weren't really there. But your attention towards me kept increasing. The next morning, you came up with a plan of going on a vacation.

"Let's soak up the Mediterranean sun, watch the sun set over Santorini, and rejuvenate the spark between us," you said, munching on your omelette.

"What happened, why a vacation suddenly?" I had asked you, sitting upright.

"Nothing, just. I know you have been stressed with a lot of work recently. Even Diya was mentioning – that your clients were taking up even your lunch breaks; did I tell you that I bumped into her the other day?"

"You met Diya? What else did she tell you?" I happened to blurt out, turning red like a thief caught red handed.

"Nothing really. Just that she was coming from Pizza by the Bay, where coincidentally she had bumped into you, lunching with a client," I could swear I noticed you looking deeper into my eyes, trying to read my reaction. Maybe I was overthinking, but then, you are after all a smart man.

"Who was he, by the way?" you asked casually.

"Just a client. What has it got to do with your vacation plan?" I almost snapped – a telltale sign of someone trying to shift the blame.

"Nothing, I was just curious. I'm glad you have someone to at least enjoy a good lunch with."

"Are you being sarcastic? Are you actually doubting me?" You wouldn't be wrong, though. But instinctively, I wanted you to be the bad guy here.

"Why are you being so defensive? I told you I was just curious. But your defensiveness belies your tale."

I stood shell-shocked for a moment, a trickle of cold sweat running down my spine. Was this it? Were you going to confront me? One part of my brain prepared some lame excuses in defense, while it readied itself for the confrontation – how could I put the entire thing on you? Thinking back to that moment now, I feel surprised as well as ashamed at how petty I was about to get with you. I never knew I had it in me to play so dirty…

"Anyways, I was here to talk about our vacation. Are you in or what? Or do you not have time for anyone aside from your clients anymore?"

You looked away as you said the above, which was a tell-tale sign that you regretted having accused me. In an instant, you were back from the doubting Yohan to the blindly-trusting-your-wife Yohan, and quickly apologised, taking back your last words. As a result, my defensiveness was also replaced by guilt, and I ended up agreeing to your proposition.

"I'll think about it," I said, and went into the kitchen, busying myself in packing lunch.

But you seemed to have made up your mind.

"Anya, listen…" you followed me in, "I think we both are in desperate need of a break – break from work, and from our mundane lives – so we can spare some time for each other. And this is the right time, too. I have been having a crazy workload, you have been having mad nights; I say we deserve this change."

"I said I will think about it, Yo."

"Why not think now? What's holding you back? Is there a problem?"

"No, there is no problem. I just need time to think about it."

"If there is no problem, then what do you need time to think about?"

I was skeptical about why you were being so pushy. I tried not to react. But I don't know what came over me – whether my guilt was too strong to hold back or was it plain disinterest that humoured me. Or if my anger at this extremely belated attempt at reviving our marriage disgusted me. Or was it all the angst from the previous day's incident involving *him*. But this time I had an outburst.

"Alright. You really want to know? Here is my answer – I have no plans of going on a vacation with you, alright? And there is no need to have this pretense now, nobody is watching us," I spoke bluntly. I know this was uncalled for. That I was overreacting, but I was unable to control myself.

"What pretense? What are you talking about?" you voiced innocently.

A huge lump – of guilt, of lost love, of a ruined marriage, of some strangely strong bond not letting me free – just surfaced all at once and I vented out as if water was gushing out of a dam's opened gates.

"Yes pretense! What else would you call this? Weren't you

the one who had cancelled this very plan when I had suggested it last year? Let me just be very clear here – this sudden interest in our relationship is not going to change things overnight. All this time, you were clueless of what in the world was going on in my life, and now, after all this while, you suddenly act as if everything is just normal between us. So, in my view, this suggestion that you are making is a little too late. I have stopped expecting any involvement from your side long ago."

As I gulped after my long monologue, I noticed you had not uttered even one comeback. I assumed your silence to be your usual avoidance approach. Exasperated at your lack of reaction, I turned and started to walk off. Suddenly, I felt you grab my hand from behind and turn me around. You looked me in the eye and said in the most gentle, genuine voice, "I had no idea my cancelling that vacation hurt you so much. Why didn't you say so before! I would've worked something out if I knew it meant so much to you." Not the response I was expecting, but there was more…

"And Anya, if I don't pester you about every small thing it does not mean that I don't think of you or worry about you. It's just that it's not my style to be the worrying man, who treats his wife as if she's a perpetual damsel in distress. And to be honest, I didn't think you would like me to be that way, would you?"

More guilt…

"Well, no. Definitely no. But it doesn't hurt to show some concern if you feel it. You cannot expect me to read your mind all the time. And seriously, you have taken your indifference to an altogether different level. I don't believe you actually cared when you acted so cold all this time. But really, what changed now? Why this sudden show of love today?"

"Why not! Look, I know I haven't been the best husband, or

in your words, 'companion' to you. And if you are honest with yourself, you know that you could have done a hundred things differently yourself. But that's beside the point. What I am trying to say is that why don't we stop digging into the past and try giving a shot to the future? We deserve that much from each other; our marriage deserves this much, doesn't it?"

Your gesture seemed honest, but with so much angst inside us, things weren't going to go back to normal with just one good talk. Even so, somewhere inside me, I knew there was merit in what you had said – that all wasn't your fault alone. And I am not referring to my relationship with *him*, but even before that, I knew deep down in my heart that I had fallen short on giving it all from my end. Perhaps, this guilt of escapism made me agree to your suggestion to a vacation. Or the guilt of possibly having been caught. Or perhaps, a tiny little corner of my heart wanted to get even with *him* for his nastiness the previous day. The age-old approach to get even with a lover – dive straight into the arms of another man (did I just think of my husband as the other man here?).

"I guess you are right," I said meekly, stepping away from him, so I did not have to meet his eye.

"So fine, let's do it. Maybe we can plan something for early next month. Does that work for you?"

"Perfect! Let me check out the package options tomorrow and we can freeze it by this weekend. I will email you once I have the quotations, cool?"

"Cool, and I will try and get the itinerary verified through Shyna – she had been there for her honeymoon earlier this year."

"Great, sounds like a plan." And with that you hugged me, ending it with a kiss this time.

I thought in my head how business-like we sounded when we

discussed any plan, but we worked perfectly like that – as a team. With *him*, though, it was different. He took the lead on matters and I could take a back seat, knowing he would plan it well. Like how he had planned our Goa trip, so perfectly. It should've made me feel good, because I did enjoy the pampering, but oddly enough, I enjoyed being part of the planning better, it made the journey more fun. All the anticipation, the efforts that went into getting the minutest details outlined – I loved all the excitement that came along with it!

And just as I thought this, I realized I was subconsciously comparing you both. The thought had never passed my mind before; after all, the two of you had belonged in different zones of my brain, not to be mingled, ever. So, this realization was quite uncomforting. I tried to shun it away, willing myself to think about it later, but the awkward feeling did not go away easily.

TANGLES

Dearest Aarav,

The next noon at work, I saw my husband's email pop up on my inbox. The subject line read, '*Santorini itinerary options*'.

True to his word, he had shared three package options along with the detailed itinerary, flight plans and costing. I had assumed his excitement the previous day was momentary and would fizzle out by night, but the detailed mail depicted his seriousness. He was not going to give up this time. I instantly called you to inform you about this latest development (you were still on your work-trip, and although we were not fighting anymore, we were still not back to complete normalcy yet). Once again, your reaction was something I could never have expected or imagined.

"Santorini sounds great. You should definitely include a visit to the Red Beach," you said simply, and I did not sense humour in your tone.

Was I annoyed or was I annoyed! I simply hung up on you. In fact, I disconnected your call when you rang back. Soon you dropped a message calling me 'getting into a meeting, speak soon,' proving my earlier assumption about your indifference.

I did not bother replying to your message. Instead, immature as it sounds, I replied to my husband confirming one of the options.

I went a step ahead and walked up to Shyna's desk. She entertained me right away – the true friend that she is! She tugged me along to the washroom so we could get some uninterrupted time. Once there, not only did she share her detailed itinerary with me, but also ended up reiterating the story of her honeymoon to me for the nth time. Yes, you know how Shyna can be so annoying at times. But she was also the one I could turn to when I needed someone to vent out to. And so, venting out I did.

After a half-hour long washroom-chat, I ended up confiding in her about us. I knew Shyna wasn't one to judge me for my extra-marital-affair, but she was surprised to see her supposedly sweet friend be involved in something as dark as this. While she joked and teased me about it, she did advise me not to mix my personal matters with office.

"Look Anya, I am the last one to advise you about your marriage, having been through a broken one myself," she said, while adding a layer of lip-gloss to her already perfect lips. "But I definitely do not want you to suffer embarrassment on the work-front because of this. Please promise me," she continued, turning around and holding my hand this time, "That you will try and sort out the E&M Foods account at the earliest. Sunendu can be quite an arse if he decides to be one, and you never know when he can use it against you."

In this, she was right. I wish I had never taken up the E&M Foods account in the first place...

Pepped up by what Shyna had told me, I was more determined get away from everything – even office. So, I looked up flight options. This time I did share the screenshots of the search results with you. I was sure this would upset you, and you would probably get back with some genuine anger this time round.

Instead, you replied with just a 'thumbs up' icon. Nothing else! What was I to make of that?

So, I went ahead and planned out the entire shebang – hotel reservations, walking tours, cruise tour – the works! I prepared a day-by-day itinerary and sent it off to my husband, keeping you in bcc. In your face mister!

Wait, I did not just send you a personal mail meant for my husband! Fuck no! I tried to immediately search online if there was a way to recall the mail…but…too late. A reply had already popped up – this time from my husband (did he not have any of his hectic workload to attend to today?) It said just four words: Whatever you say, darling :)

Darling! I stared at that word for a minute. First, it had been very long since my husband had called me that, so it felt somewhat awkward. I realized how awkward it might be with him on the actual vacation if we do go for it. I felt my heart race a bit at the thought, and then maybe, by some auto-defense mechanism, I shunned it away and my mind directed the thoughts in another, more pleasant direction – one of sipping wine at Red Beach…

I waited all day to hear back from you. The more I thought of it, the more childish my actions seemed to me. And the guilt of leading on my husband in the way that I did – so wrong! Unfortunately, I was unable to find a way out of this mess despite overthinking it so much. I could have made a last-minute excuse to him, as always, and called off the vacation. But my mind kept going back to this tiny bother at the back of my mind that you had been unaffected by this entire episode. Not only had you not apologized for your earlier behaviour, but also now, you had topped it with your indifference. Here I was, feeling humiliated at office, guilt-trapped at home and ignored outside of home. But none of these seemed to bother you in the least. It seemed extremely rude to me that you would act, or rather not act, like this.

Well, I decided to make the move myself, and give you a call. It was around eleven in the night. Should I take the chance of speaking with you from my home? I had not done that before today, and it seemed like an unnecessary risk. Yet, the anxiety was killing me, and I had to get this sorted. I had had a hard time dodging the topic of bookings the entire evening, pretending to act super busy with work, and it would be difficult to avoid it another day after the excitement I had myself created. I could not take this any longer. Speaking to you was the only way of putting my head at ease. But the question was how?

I tiptoed out of the room, taking my laptop in hand, ready to make another work-excuse should my husband wake up. I set up the laptop on the living room sofa and stepped into the balcony with the phone to make sure I was out of hearing range, ready to pretend to be on a work-call should my husband walk in on me.

You did not receive it the first time around. Perhaps, you were asleep already, I thought. But no, how could you sleep so easily when I was so restless? I dialed your number again. This time you received it, mentioned you had had a hectic day, and were exhausted. Well, tired or not, we were going to have the talk now!

"You seem to be sleeping really well, I see," I taunted. "Well, I guess that means you are fine with my vacation plan."

"You really want to talk about this now? Is that why you called? Stop acting childish, Anya," you snapped.

"Excuse me! Forgive me for being the only one here to be worried restless about spending a romantic vacation with my husband. If your sleep is so much more important to you, then I

put our leftover awkwardness instantly at ease. For the first time in the last twenty-four hours, we shared a comforting hug. I won't lie to you – there was comfort there, in your – my husband's – arms. It took me away from all the guilt and the angst I felt towards him.

Something in your own stance told me that you were feeling the same. I tried to question if you were okay, but you made light of the topic saying you just felt bad that we had to have such an ugly conversation to land at a place so beautiful. So simple, but so true. The path to happiness often treads through sad alleys. The path to *him* treaded through unfaithfulness…

I shrugged to take my mind off him and focused instead on the interiors of our villa. The whitewashed walls typical of Santorini were more beautiful in person than in the pictures. I especially loved the villa you had booked for us – this two-storied beauty. The living room on the ground had French windows that opened into an infinity pool leading into the sea (you had splurged on this one – I could see that). I couldn't get over the spiral stairs going up to the bedroom, which was round in shape, no edges or nooks whatsoever! The bedroom with its full-length French windows gave a spellbinding view of the dark sea on a starry night. Adjoining the master bed was the Jacuzzi, which seemed so enticing after the tiring journey that I decided right away to not keep it waiting any longer, dived right in. Lazy as we were, we agreed to call-in for dinner that day, before you decided to join me. The only thing that kept us from getting intimate that night was our exhaustion. But I knew I was not going to be able to dodge it for the remaining holiday…

The next day we donned on our sunhats and set out to explore the shore on foot. The narrow alleys were crowded with tourists and sellers selling the typical things that were attractive to tourists. We indulged ourselves in a bit of shopping, then scouted the neighborhood a bit, then dined at a local taverna (wasn't the octopus delicious!) and roamed around a bit more. Come evening, we decided to have a drink at the corner bar. That was when the conversation I had been dreading popped up.

"So how are things at work? You don't talk much about it these days," you asked casually.

"It's good, hectic mostly. Hardly have the time to talk at the end of the day," I tried to be casual too.

"Yeah, I've noticed you have been super busy. Who's that new client you are handling?"

"Oh no, don't get started on it again!" I tried to get the upper hand.

"No, I'm not. Seriously. I just don't know about any of your other clients to talk about. What's his name by the way?"

I know you are a smart man. I knew at that point it was your insecurity speaking. I had to be smarter.

"It's E&M Foods. They are planning to give us the account for their entire foods portfolio, and Sunendu wants me to lead it. It's big, as you can guess. Hence, so much pressure," I replied like a professional, keeping his name out completely.

You replied with a non-committal 'hmm', figuring it was going to be tough extracting anything more out of me. So instead, you diverted the topic to about us.

"Anya, I have been meaning to bring this up since a while now, just haven't been getting the chance to. I have a confession to make," you said seriously. I gulped, fearing what was going to come up next.

"That day, I did in fact take Diya seriously and doubted you. For a moment, I did think you were seeing this guy. It made me so jealous, I wanted to find him and punch him in the face. I was super mad at you as well, and initially, I thought I should just confront you head on. But then, I recalled the promises we made to each other – about being each other's best friends and companions. I could not doubt you even for a minute, Anya. I am sorry I did."

I could not believe what you had just said. I was so shocked; I was left speechless.

But you continued, "To be frank, I think it was my own insecurity that was at play. We both know we haven't been on the best of terms of late, in fact for a while now, if we are to be honest. But believe me when I say this – this marriage means the world to me. I want to make it work, and I am ready to put in the works."

You held my hand at this point, and I can't say it felt as awkward as earlier. Your confession made me cry at the back of my throat, whereas your intent to work on the marriage set me restless. The fact that you did have reason to doubt me, the fact that you did think about it, after all, and the fact that you chose to get over it and lay your trust in me despite all of this – it was enough to make me want to confess myself. But all I could muster the courage for was to hold your hand and rest my head on your shoulders. I wished then, to turn back time and take back all the harsh things I had ever said to you. You were indeed undeserving of the betrayal I was putting you through, and I was about to blurt out…

Just then you enveloped me in your arms and hushed me quiet. Your soft tone had a relaxing effect on my exhausted, overworked nerves. Inadvertently, I let my head rest in the hollow of your shoulder and held your hand tighter, and that was how we walked around the rest of the evening.

I must admit, I was enjoying the evening being my old self with my husband. You were back to being your adventurous self and proposed a hike up to the Skaros Rock. I reverted at being my sporty self too and took up the offer more than happily. We treaded along the curvy, narrow alleys of Fira, making it just in time to catch the sunset from the top of the fort.

The view from the top was spell bounding. Sapphire waves lashed onto the pearl whites of Santorini houses, adorning it in a necklace of a splash where the rock met the sea. The yellow haze of the setting sun surrounded the charming Aegean in a halo, which in turn glowed like a dame who blushes under her lover's gaze.

The picture was a perfect no-filter-needed postcard takeaway. You planted a kiss on my cheek to seal the moment.

When the sun finally bid its goodbye for the day, it rendered the evening in a peaceful quiet. We walked back to our villa in this quiet, not wanting to disturb the serenity with our words. Once there, the wine awaited us, and we took it up to the Jacuzzi. Quickly we undressed into our underwear and stepped in. Romantically, we raised our glasses to a toast.

"To finding back our old selves, and to celebrating our new start," you announced, and drank up. It was only a moment before we found ourselves kissing each other.

A splatter of rain poured then. The rains hold such magic as to render even a simpleton romanticize everything around him. I was no different. Whether it was the natural ease of being with you or the wine working its charm, whether it was guilt of keeping you away for so long or an obligation that I owed, whether it was *his* want disguised in some unknown form or just some unknown emotion crawling its way up, I know not. But when you initiated what the kiss had started, I let my guard down.

I felt your tongue find its way to mine, as your hand slid down to my breast. I held you by the hair to bring you closer to me and arched my body up to meet yours. We rocked in sync to the lapping waves of the Jacuzzi and splashing drops of rain. You then lifted me up and carried me in your arms to the bed. I could see the raw hunger in your eyes, and it only seduced me to get on top of you. I bit your ears lightly and worked my way down. You held me by my hair and moaned in pleasure; then pulled me up and swung me around to put yourself on top now. You gazed at me and lay a final kiss on my lips before leading me to that ultimate rapture.

The next morning you woke up with a sprint in your walk, me – the opposite. Having realized the full-blown effect of what I had allowed myself into, I was on tenterhooks of losing my mind. Fuck!

As you walked around the room bare chested, reading aloud the plan for the rest of the day from the itinerary saved on your phone, I tried to wrap my head around what I should be doing, what I should be saying, and most importantly, what I should be feeling. As an instinct, I tried to think of ways in which I could apologize to you for the false hope I had clearly raised in you, for regardless of how bad my fight with him was or how great our last night's sex was, I still loved *him* so. Yet, I only remember the glint in your eyes that showed genuine happiness after ages. As I moved about avoiding your gaze, you talked about the history of Santorini. I have no idea how I managed to remember you mentioning that Santorini was earlier known as Thera and was essentially built by layers of lava from three significant volcanic eruptions. Perhaps, a trick of the mind to manage stress?

Regardless, I could not bring myself to dampen your spirits and so, went ahead with the day displaying a fake excitement all along. I only vaguely recall the six hundred-step walk down to the Old Port. That day, even the tranquil beauty of the place failed to lift my mood. We posed for several selfies together, gulped down the delicious meal that you clearly ravished – moussaka and taramasalata with bread and olives, worth ravishing indeed – and fibbed about how exciting the entire trip was turning out to be.

Only later that evening I realized the urgency of the matter when you, clearly still overjoyed by the revived spark of our marriage, once again broached the topic of family planning.

"Anya, I am so glad we have been able to get past our differences. Had I known that a vacation could do such wonders, I would have never denied it in the first place. My sincere apologies to you, darling.

"However, having said that, I am glad we are here today. And with the way things are going, I am confident that we will be great parents to a cute, little kid."

I tried to protest instantly, you held your finger up to my lips and interrupted me, "Now, before you protest, let me tell you, that it is just my request to you to consider it once. No pressure whatsoever. And I promise, regardless of what you decide, I will love you just as much as I do today, in this moment." You moved your finger down to my chin and used it to pull my face closer to yours, so you could plant a kiss on my lips.

"You know, Anya, I would like you to know something. The last couple of days have made me realize a few things. The most important being the reason we married in the first place. You and I are great together, we always have been! We just need to work on our stubbornness, the alpha personalities that you keep saying we both are, haha!"

I knew that beneath the light you were making of matters, you were damn serious about every word you spoke. I had no choice but to keep silent.

"Anya, I know I don't say it often, but I do love you, my dear. And I have only felt the emotion grow stronger in the last couple of days. You have no idea how much joy it has brought me to see you be yourself again – to be goofy and adventurous with you all over again. And that's what made me realize, that regardless of whether we have a child or not, what I would want most is to just not lose you again. So, it is my promise to you, Mrs Anya Yohan Arora, that I will never take you away from you ever again, that I will respect you and your decisions always, and I will love you for you – forever and always."

The kiss after this was longer, deeper. The pang of guilt that followed was to be even more lingering.

I knew I would be entering a jumble maze if I acted on my next thought, but I couldn't help assuring you, holding your hand a tad bit tighter, if only to keep your heart from shattering too soon.

And that was how we spent the remaining two days of our stay there – roaming the alleys hand-in-hand, soaking up the Aegean sun, relishing the exotic delicacies and drinking up the woos in wines. The museums, the sea, the taverns, the fort – all of it seemed more enticing when I convinced my mind to think only of keeping you happy in the moment, for the moment – the rest could be dealt with later.

DISCLOSURE

Dearest Aarav,

We returned to Mumbai on Sunday evening. The rest of the day was spent unpacking stuff. The magnets were put up on the fridge, our living room had a new tile-pot that would soon need a plant, and the postcards were taped on to the wine bottles and kept aside to be given away as gifts. Laundry came next – and my husband and I worked in sync as usual. Dinner was ordered in, and exhausted as we were we dozed off the second the lights were out.

Soon, I told myself as a last thought that night, I would need to broach the topic and come clean to my husband.

That morning I found my husband rushing about the house. He had an early morning meeting and was out of the house before I even got to the breakfast table. I thanked the stars for the alone time.

It allowed me to plan about how I could explain things to him.

Office was hectic that day, as work had piled on over the course of the last five days. I had planned to take some time out to speak with you, but I was so overwhelmed with tasks that I was unable to spare any moment to find time to even call you. So, our 'chat' would have to wait. One thing I was sure of though, I wanted to speak with you before speaking with my husband.

Fortunately, my husband got home even later than I did that evening – and that is something, given I reached home only around ten in the night. But unlike before, I now had frequent messages from him updating me not just about himself and his schedule, but also checking in on me and my whereabouts. The surprise was when he messaged to ask about my dinner – now that was a first. This was not a good sign. The nicer he got, the more and more nervous I became. I needed to get the guilt out of my system, and that would need some quiet time in person.

However, as luck would have it, the next few days were no different and were spent with just brief sightings of each other.

On the brighter side, the work environment seemed to have improved since I was back. Sunendu was busy with his other account, which had apparently been stuck in design at our end. As a result, he was in too much of a mess himself to bother about anyone else. Animesh, on the other hand, had roped me in on a global pitch for Dew Beverages, another large and important client, so the topic of E&M Foods was on a back burner for him. The time away indeed seemed to have done its job, at least on this front.

The pitch for Dew Beverages was an exciting one, being one of the few global accounts my company received. So, expectedly, the stakes were running high. Converting this one was not going to be easy. As a result, there were a lot many long nights lined up until pitch-day.

Honestly, I couldn't complain. First, I loved the work – it was challenging, it stood potential to get me the visibility I deserved and not to mention, the adrenaline rush that came along with such fast-paced, high-stakes projects. Second, the crazy workload meant I had a ready excuse to keep my mind off the mess on the personal front. It also helped that you were not back in town yet from your tour. For that matter, my husband was tied up with his own business-as-usual, implying he was unlikely to have respite from the crazy load for a few days at least.

With the personal front sorted, I was able to focus better on my pitch. I recovered my zeal to deliver my best – leading from the front and collaborating with the other teams seamlessly. We started having fun as a team. Most fun were the brainstorming sessions, where the entire team would gang up to come up with the so-called 'out of the box' ideas. Now, with a bunch of youngsters dominating the space, these sessions often ended up being nothing short of a laugh riot, not to mention, the endless flow of caffeine, on-demand supply of pizzas, and an occasional allowance of beer-at-work. What more could one ask from a job!

Time often flies when one is enjoying oneself. That's exactly what happened here as well. Without much notice, three weeks went by and pitch-day was here. Animesh, the rest of the team and I, were perked up to present our best work until date to the client. Surely, we were nervous, but also confident. As a result, we were able to defend our plan to them perfectly.

Our hard work paid off, and how! The project was ours, and the company bagged an exclusive sign-up from the client for three years. Now that's how it is done.

I was exhilarated and exhausted at the same time. Now, I was ready to face the challenges in the other facet of my life. I decided to confess as soon as possible to my husband and was confident

I would be able to explain our scenario to him well. I knew he would be upset, and I deserved it too, but I was also sure he would eventually understand my side of the story and forgive me. Yet, the thought of leaving him high and dry made my heart cringe…

I tried to divert my mind, and it was drawn to you. I was so ready to come to you and unwind in your arms. It was time for us to resolve all issues as well. I knew I still had to tell you about the Santorini 'incident' with my husband, but if there was anybody who could understand the situation well, it had to be you. I knew I had to see you and see you soon.

I arrived at your place at around eight in the evening. I was thoroughly exhausted from the crazy evenings of the week gone by, but the thought of seeing you after so long spruced me up. You were quick to answer the door, and boy, did I underestimate the joy of seeing you after so long! Add to it, you looked hot even in your tracks and a casual, short-sleeved t-shirt that showed off your muscular arms perfectly. The V-neck of your tee led the path from your neck to chest, with the bump of your Adam's apple coursing up-and-down rhythmically. You were some hot stuff, for sure!

I had to shake myself back to focus. This wasn't the right moment to fantasize about your body. We were meeting after a very long span, and there were matters to be sorted. To start with, we needed to clear the mess about the work deal we were part of – the one that led to all this mess in the first place.

You led me in with a warm smile, and did not wait to embrace me in a warm, tight hug the instant I was in. Looking up at your bespectacled eyes, I saw the sweet smile that had a disarming effect on me every time I laid eyes on them. Forgotten was my angst and lost were my worries when you smiled that smile of yours.

"Gosh, how I missed you!" you initiated, as you scooped me up and placed me on the sofa, with your arm still around me.

"That's a good start to an apology," I reverted, pretending to still be angry about our fight.

"Ha-ha! Alright, if I must…I am sorry to have avoided you, ma'am. How do you want me to apologize?" you were quick to comply, adding kisses on my neck to show your intent.

"Yes, that will help…" I stretched out to give you more of me.

"Really, now! Is that how angry you are?"

"You have no idea," I teased back.

You accepted the challenge, and we made out right there, on your sofa.

Half an hour later, we were back to being sober. We headed to the dining table whereupon you brought out the wine glasses. As you ordered pizza through the delivery app, I soaked in your image once more – you were all back-to-business with the focused look. Only I had the eye to notice the slight twitch at the corner of your eyes when you tried to seek the perfect option. You did not have a smile on your face, but only I could have noticed the slight curve when you caught my gaze on you. You had the chiseled look that could send heat waves up a girl's spine, but only I noticed the softness beneath through your gentle kisses. I saw more in you than you possibly were, and only I could place you on the pedestal of the perfect lover that you probably weren't.

That thought reminded me of your stance on my work, and the fact that we had not really resolved the matter yet. So, I brought it up, knowing all too well that any venting I might put onto you on this matter was likely to come biting back at me when I disclose my Santorini endeavor. Hopefully, I had a resolution to everything?

"So, Aarav," I initiated, "we never really discussed the entire E&M Foods deal fiasco after our fight. If you ask me, I am still a little mad at you for the way you reacted."

"I know, baby, I was a little harsh. But you need to understand that sometimes, you need to ignore the gossip mongers and just grasp the opportunity."

"I am sorry, what? What do you mean by grasping the opportunity? Firstly, personal and professional life must be kept separate. And secondly, in such a scenario as ours, the comment was so derogatory by itself, let alone associating it with my work and implying taking advantage of the situation!"

"You are getting me wrong, sweetheart," you seemed to be calm today, unlike me – who was a wreck of nerves with a million thoughts sabotaging my mind.

"What I am trying to say," you explained, "is that people are bound to comment either way. So why let an opportunity go by?"

At this, I took a deep breath. While on one hand, you did have a point, on the other, you still did not get it!

"I don't think we are going to see eye-to-eye on this matter. Guess we will just have to agree to disagree," I decided to close the chapter, as I had things that were more important to talk about.

You too seemed to have put the matter behind you already. "Come here, now, my idealist sweetheart," you hugged me once again; "There will always be issues that we will not agree upon. What matters is that we are still on the same page when it comes to one crucial matter – the matter of our hearts."

Hearing you get all romantic made my heart beat faster. There was no more beating around the bush.

"Aarav, I have a confession to make," I muttered softly.

While the smile on your face did not diminish, I noticed your stance go straight upon hearing the word 'confession'.

Here it comes…

"While we were in Fira, I had sex with my husband." There, I said it. It wasn't the first time I had had sex with my husband after meeting you, although it surely was the first time I was letting you know of it. I tried to wonder why…

You looked at me blankly. It must have been just a moment, but a thousand thoughts crossed my mind in that split second. How I had planned to say it differently, how I had thought of explaining to you what led up to the moment and how guilty I felt after, how I had wanted to tell you that none of it mattered…

Instead, I just left it at that. And waited.

"Oh," was all you said after that moment.

"I won't lie – I half expected it. Or rather, half dreaded it. I don't know what led you to do it, nor do I want to know. No, please don't tell me anymore about it. I won't be able to take it," you turned away, perhaps to hide your flushing red anger at the vision that you had built in your head of me in bed with my husband. I knew that was what you had pictured; I knew you had.

"I can't tell you how restless I had been the entire duration you were away with him. I know I did not show it to you, but I sure, as hell was unable to get a single good night's sleep thinking of you at an exotic location with the man who has a legal right over you. Perhaps, this is my punishment for holding up my ego so high."

You were still averting your eye. I know your heart was shattering inside, shattering even more with each passing moment.

"I wish you hadn't told me, Anya. I really do," and you turned away from me.

"I am so sorry!" I cried out as I hugged you. "It has been killing me all this time. I don't know what to say. I am just so, so sorry!" Now I was teary too.

You turned around and hid me in your arms.

"Hush, now. I know you did not mean it. But it still hurts. I can't lose you again, Anya. I won't ever let you go away," You pulled up my face in both your palms and kissed me a million kisses.

"It is behind us now. I promise not to talk about it ever again."

I muffled a million promises into your shoulder as I buried myself in you, and you shed your tears in my hair, as you gripped me closer about.

"I don't think I can share you with him anymore," you said, breaking the silence after a long while.

"I know," I told you then, "I will tell him about us very soon."

But at the back of my mind, I had no idea how to break it to him. A part of me wanted to never let him know, just so that he could be spared the hurt and the pain. A part of me wanted to never let him know also because it knew well that seeing *him* in pain would pain *me* also just as much…

We stayed cozily in each other's arms in the quiet for a while afterwards, forgetting the world, knowing only each other. Tomorrow was going to be a different day, we knew. But today, this was good. This was good enough.

Laying in your arms, I couldn't help but think about how complicated life had gotten. I guess we had reached the point where extra marital affairs become tricky – a point which we had been delusional in believing we would never arrive at – for we were happy where we had been, not expecting, not demanding. But of course, expectations are like dreams. They reside in your subconscious and show up when you are either most at ease or most at stress! Their arrival brings with it the web of lies and guilt and passion and love, a web that entangles you such that it leaves no way out of it without breaking the threads that bind it – in this case, the threads of relations. And yet, despite knowing all this, one always thinks that the situation can be dealt-with with some care and caution, not realizing how some situations don't really have a way to be dealt with. As they say, finding a solution through tricky lanes often leads to dead-ends. Or in such cases, dead relationships.

While I pondered over ways to cause minimum damage, my silly mind did not understand that there was not going to be anything "minimum" about the damage I was about to cause…to all of us.

CONFESSION

Dearest Yohan,

It was the dawn of the next day. The day I was to let you know about him and me. The day you were going to remember for the rest of your life, as the day you stopped loving, the day you stopped trusting. For what kind of a woman would go about leading a man that she does not intend to be with?

You hugged me a goodbye as you left for office that morning, as you had been doing every day since our return from Greece. You reminded me that you would be returning early today, and that we should make it a date night. You turned back then, to tell me you would be cooking me a special meal at home instead.

Jitters ran down my spine when I saw the gleam in your eyes. I shivered at the mere thought of confronting you. Half-hour later, I found myself staring at the text from you that said you were looking forward to our date-night. A heart emoji followed. Yohan Arora was using heart emojis in his messages to me. What had I done to you?

I went about office absent-mindedly. I had gulped down three cups of cappuccino already and was on my way to grab a fourth from the breakout area of the office. After all, the sinking feeling that the thought confrontation had brought about was not going to settle down easily. I pondered, sipping on the piping hot coffee, as to how it was comparatively easier for me to resolve the most challenging problems at work, but come personal front and I was no better at facing my demons than a novice intern struggling to barely stay afloat on his first day at work.

Shyna must have seen me frequenting the coffee vending machine, so she walked up to me. It felt so good to finally have someone to speak my heart out to, that I narrated the entire story to her – right from my history with *him* to *our* present, and the big question that stood before me now: how to let you know about me and *him*. As always, she was the voice of my conscience that I feared but needed, yet often ignored.

"Are you sure you want to confess to Yohan? And are you absolutely sure about Aarav? And are you absolutely sure you do not love Yohan at all?"

"Of course, Shyna. What kind of a question is that?"

"I mean if 'Sex in Santorini' is anything to go by, then maybe you still have lingering feelings about Yohan, and probably you are just finding some recluse in Aarav…"

"I have thought about it, Shyna," I defended impulsively, "I love Aarav. I always have. I don't think I really ever got over him. Perhaps, that was why I had never been able to go ahead and make a family with Yohan. At the same time, Yo does not deserve this. He has been anything but nice to me. We still share a special bond – he is my person! I can't keep him in the dark anymore. I can't lead him on like this. I will die of guilt if I see him do one more sweet gesture for me."

"I get what you are trying to say. And I know you are coming from a good place. But Anya, there is no going back from this. Up until now, the ball was in your court. Difficult as the choice might be, you could choose to play it or pass it. But after your confession, you will be entering the point of no return."

"I know. Hence the jitters. Pray for me Shyna!"

"I will, always. I am here if you need me."

"Thanks, Shyna. I love you, babes."

✳ ✳ ✳

That night, as I entered the house, you welcomed me with a cheerful smile and a warm hug. You had the ambience set for our date night – dim lights, expensive chinaware lay neatly on the table, a plate of sautéed mushrooms and scrumptious looking roasted chicken sat temptingly by its side, a white wine bottle was out laying in the ice bucket, waiting to be popped open.

"Welcome home, Mrs Arora. You seem to have had a very hectic day," you said cheerfully. You did notice the exhaustion on my face, but clearly mistook it for work stress.

"Would you care for some wine, to help you relax?" you poured the wine as you spoke and handed me the flute.

I took it, still dazed with the entire set up. You had made it all the more difficult for me to break it to you.

"I need to speak with you, Yohan."

"Yes, my dear. I am all yours. And we have the entire night in front of us to talk. So, for now, why don't you start with the sautéed mushrooms?"

"Yohan, thank you for all this. But you really shouldn't have," I started with the apology for your efforts – simple things first.

"Why not? You deserve it," you chimed cheerfully.

"No, I don't."

You still thought I was trying to play it down, be modest or whatever. And so, you ignored my comment and continued with your 'date-mode'.

"Anyhow, tell me about your day. Was it that bad?"

I nodded, as it was true, after all.

"Fancy a head massage?" You are unbelievable, I thought. The more I try to be distant with you, the more difficult you were making it for me.

"Yohan, please. I really need to talk to you about something," I insisted a little strongly this time.

"Can't even wait for after dinner? The chicken will get cold…"

"Please?"

"Alright. Tell me, what is it?"

Hmm, this was it. Where do I begin?

"Yo, I know you are trying very hard to get things back to where they were at the beginning. But you really shouldn't be spending your energy on me. The thing is we are not on the same page in this matter."

I paused to check your reaction – you were gradually withdrawing yourself but didn't seem to have guessed where I was going with this.

"Not on the same page meaning…?"

"That I…well, I can't …I mean, I am not…" I simply couldn't find the right words to cause minimum hurt.

"You are not ready to be a mom? Is that what you are trying to say? Listen Anya, I already told you, I am okay to wait until you are ready, if at all you are ever ready. You don't need to feel pressured by all this."

Were you the same man I had married? When did you turn so understanding, so calm? Where was the Yohan I knew? I know you had changed significantly, but to not find any traces of your older self, especially on matters so close to your heart was shocking even to me.

This Yohan was different than the Yohan I had been living with since the last two years. This Yohan was kind, understanding, and respectful. And he genuinely cared.

I was trying hard to see through you – to find that faint line of flaw, a hint that you still had an ounce of arrogance and chauvinism in you – so I could be spared from feeling so pathetic.

But I failed. You were indeed a changed man. A likeable man. A man I would have never fallen out of terms with, had you been this way all along. Why did it have to be this way? Why did you have to change now, after everything?

I held both your hands in mine and met your gaze so I could finally tell you. But the softness in your eyes took me back to the good times we had once shared…

The memory of our wedding *pheras* came to my mind. You in your pearl white sherwani, and me in the rose-red lehenga, walking around the sacred fire, hands linked, promising our endless support to each other…

The memory of you putting the *sindoor* on my forehead, and the *mangalsutra* around my neck, committing to each other for seven lives…

The memory of the vows we made to each other. Vows that I failed at keeping, and yet, they created a bond so strong that guilt overwhelms me when I even consider letting it loose. Do I have it in me to endure this guilt for life? Perhaps, not.

"I cannot do this anymore!" I blurted out, tears flowing down my cheeks.

"I am sorry, I really am, but I can't put you through this. I don't deserve you!" I burst out crying now.

You were clearly taken aback. You knew now that something was terribly wrong, but you still wouldn't have guessed the extent of the wrong, so naturally, you tried to pacify me.

"It's alright. Stop crying first. Here, have some water."

I pushed away the glass you were offering me and continued sobbing instead.

"You need to calm down first. Anya! Look at me, look at me and tell me clearly what the matter is." You grabbed me by the shoulder, albeit gently, half pacifying, half questioning.

In between the sobs, I managed to finally mutter the words, "I am seeing someone else…"

That did it.

I no longer felt your hands on me. I no longer felt the genteel in your stance. I did, however, feel your stare – a cold, aloof, glaring stare.

"Are you kidding me?"

"I am sorry…"

"What the hell do you mean you are sorry? What is all this? Am I a fool to do all this for you – to arrange all this, to go on a vacation with you…" you trailed off, as if just realizing something…

"Since when?" you asked simply.

"I am sorry…" was all I could say.

"Since when?" you were sterner now.

"A while…"

"What do you mean by a while? Were you sleeping with

someone else while holidaying with me in Greece?"

The disgust in your voice was very evident now.

"I am sorry, I didn't mean to..."

"Of course, you meant to. Please don't give me this crap about how sorry you are. All this while you made me believe that we were getting back on track, when in fact you were just trying to make yourself feel good. That's all it was, wasn't it?" you snapped.

I had no answer to your accusation.

"Really, what kind of a person does this? I mean, gosh! What do I even make of this?" You were pacing around the room now, running your hands through your hair now, clearly angry, frustrated.

"Just listen to me, please. I beg you. I really didn't want to hurt you..." I begged you, all the while crying ceaselessly.

"No! No, Anya. I do not want to listen to you anymore. I just feel like a royal, fucking fool right now."

"No, please don't say that."

"It is that client of yours, isn't it?" Your stare was venomous now. I had never seen you so furious before. Your angst scared me to the core.

"I knew it. I should have believed Diya when she tried to tell me. But instead, like a stupid fool that I am, I go and trust your fake stories instead," you vented out, throwing the water glass that you had offered me just minutes ago.

I shrieked in fear at the sound of the crashing glass, crumbling up my feet onto the chair. I was really, really scared now. This was much worse than anything I had imagined. And only I was to be blamed for it.

"You know what, Anya? Had you said this to me a month ago,

I would probably not have hated you so much. But you had to lead me on to finally make me believe we stood a chance to be happy together before giving me this blow. How sick can you be?"

"Yo, please. I am sorry. I meant to tell you sooner, I just didn't have the heart to…"

"Stop it!" You said, walking off. "You disgust me." You banged the main door in my face as you left.

REMINISCENCE

Dearest Yohan,

I sat on the floor sobbing helplessly, staring at the door you had shut in my face. I had done what I had been dreading the most. I had broken you for my selfish needs and broken you when you were most vulnerable.

This was not how I had planned things to be. Nothing was how I had planned it to be. You and I weren't meant to be at such odds with each other. When we had first met, I would have never guessed we were capable of causing each other so much pain...

You do remember how we met for the first time, don't you? One might call it a typical arranged-marriage set-up. But for us, it was the beginning of the rest of our lives.

✳ ✳ ✳

When I had okayed the profile of the prospective guy – Punjabi, MBA, investment banker – that my dad had dug out from the community's marriage bureau, I had not imagined things to progress so smoothly. He had reached out to your dad, who had tallied our *'kundalis'* and when they apparently matched very well, had agreed to arrange an in-person meeting for the 'girl and guy'.

Thus, the girl and the guy had been given each other's numbers to decide on the time and place to meet. The girl was instructed to not initiate, the guy had to make the first move. And the guy did. The first conversation was very reticent, both of them keeping things cordial – for both of them had experienced failures of such arranged set-ups earlier and saw no point in getting over-friendly at get go. A short intro, a quick check on availability over the weekend, a brief discussion on what location would be mid-way from both their places and a few options of cafes to pick from. The succinct chat resulted in the boy and the girl meeting at 5 pm, on Sunday, at Starbucks Café in Powai.

They both reached the venue at around the same time. In fact, they bumped into each other at the parking lot itself.

"It's Anya, right?" were the first words you had said to me as you walked next to me on the pavement towards the café. You must have recognized me from my profile picture. I was not dressed very differently for the occasion as such – an orange sleeveless chiffon dress that reached my calves, with a brown belt to tame its flowing form and matching brown kitten heels to go with it.

I was at first taken aback with the suddenness of a stranger talking to me in the middle of a road, but I recognized you from the picture in your profile.

"Yohan? Hi!" I held out my hand, using the other to tame my flying hair. You shook my hand firmly. I liked your confidence right there. You stood tall at five-seven and matched my five-five frame well. I tried to second-guess your persona from your attire – checkered brown shirt with rolled up sleeves that flaunted a Rado watch on a stable wrist, beige chinos and grey loafers. You had a light stubble that was well trimmed, and wore an after-shave that was not too strong, nor too mild. Your square jawline betrayed the soft mouth that had a warm smile that reached your eyes. Honest eyes, I remember thinking.

"That's right. Perfect timing, I must say," you smiled.

"Indeed. I like that you are punctual," I bit my tongue for complimenting you too soon.

"In fact, I must say that for you, given how women like to be fashionably late!"

We both giggled at the vile attempt to humour and headed inside to an empty table.

"Hope you did not encounter too much traffic on your way down," you initiated the conversation.

"Not really, which explains why I was able to make it on time," I smiled.

"True, true…" the conversation was on the verge of getting awkward. I thought in my head, if it got awkward, it would be another one of the many wasted Sundays.

"I am not a fan of driving in Mumbai traffic as such. Cab sharing is much more time-efficient," you tried to carry on the conversation.

"I totally agree, get to have some much needed off-time while on the road if you aren't driving yourself," I added.

"Plus, I can't stand putting my legs through the torture of an hour-long exercise after torturing the mind for an entire day!"

Not bad, I thought, as I laughed at your second attempt of the day. You might have been bad at humour, but you definitely scored points on putting me at ease instantly.

"So, hot or cold?" you asked, concerning our order.

"Hot always, cappuccino preferably, ideally dry. How about you?"

"Cold always, with cream and sprinkles on top."

We nodded at each other, the difference in our choices sinking in. Nothing significant, but it was a start. Need to find out more, I was thinking, when you said, "Let's continue finding out more of our similarities and differences after placing the order…" you said, as you walked up to the counter to give the details in the exact fashion as I had spelled them out.

"So, are you ready?"

"Bring it on!" I said.

"Mountains or beach?" you asked.

"Beach. You?"

"Beach. Your turn."

"Party all night or Netflix and Chill?"

"Fridays for party and weekends for chill. You?"

"Perfect! I think I will go with what you just said. Your turn."

"Money, money, honey or happiness is the true wealth?"

"Happiness is the true wealth after you have accumulated sufficient money, honey!"

"I like that!" you said, laughing at my presumably better sense of humor. I went ahead with the next one "Okay, this one is important. A perfect ten or beauty is in the flaws?"

"If it is about me, I need to be a perfect ten. For everyone else, flaws all the way, and as Chris Martin says…let me fix you!"

"Wow! Finally, mister. You did catch up on your humour

quotient. High-five for that," and we exchanged a high-five!

"So, a last one, to decide our next move – dine-out or order-in?"

"Sassy, aren't you? How about a cook-in? And make it special."

You laughed out loud this time. "Not bad, not bad! I shall keep this in mind," and you teased. And just like that, we were at it already. Smooth…

I knew we would get along well, but I had to make sure there was no misunderstanding later. So, I diverted the topic in a somewhat serious direction.

"So Yo, tell me this," I started, but you interrupted me. "Yo? I like the sound of that. I guess I can get used to it," you smiled a smile that made me blush.

I continued, "Listen, I think we both realize we are compatible. But I want to just clarify a few things before we proceed to a more serious stage."

"You want to talk about our respective pasts, isn't it?"

I was taken aback with your sharp implication. I knew then that you were a smart man who knew the ways of the world.

"Well, yes. I want you to know that until a year ago, I was deeply in love with a guy for some time. When things did not work out between us, it took me a long time to get back to being myself. I think this is important for you to know, since it tells you that I tend to be very emotional about the people I attach myself to. At the same time, the breakup taught me that I needed to have a more practical approach to life. And so, when I decided to look for a partner for my life, I promised myself to prioritize mutual respect and compatibility over emotional or physical attraction, because relationships can be challenging, and only love may not be sufficient to sustain them."

"Anya, firstly, I appreciate you being so candid about everything. I like the fact that you are not overlooking the practical challenges a marriage is likely to bring. Let me tell you two things here. First that I am a hundred percent in agreement that marriage is much more than just love. It is much more demanding and likely to ask for a lot more than just emotional support from your spouse. So, I can say this for myself at least, that I am first looking to find a friend – preferably a best friend at that – and then a spouse."

I liked how you had summarized everything. It spoke a lot about your maturity, something I grew up to value in you over the course of time.

You continued, "Secondly, we all have our pasts. Honestly, I don't think we are truly grown until we have faced at least one failure in the subject of 'love-ology'," you said, rolling your eyes, "I have also been in a couple of relationships myself. Except, I did not see my future in either of them. So, in my case, neither of them lasted very long. But then, the onus is on me for that one!" You smiled humbly with that closing statement.

We chatted for about an hour more, talking about everything under the sun – our jobs, our goals and aspirations, our dream house, bucket lists – everything. At the end of the day, we both knew we would be giving a go ahead to our respective parents back home. And boy, were they overjoyed or what!

We continued talking for a few more weeks after that, meeting a couple more times in the interim. Our fondness for each other grew with each conversation we had. We discovered that we were not just similar in our temperaments, but also in our backgrounds. My mom was into railways, while your dad worked with Air India. My dad was the head of department for the mechanical engineering department, at the Delhi Technological University, while your mom was an academician as well with an education startup. We had both spent a couple of years of our early school life in boarding and had both moved out of house since our engineering days. As if this wasn't enough, the one that I couldn't ignore was the fact that I had lived in Kirti Nagar until my schooling, whereas your family had shifted there upon completion of your schooling. With such similar background, it became easier to relate to you and compatibility came naturally. Soon enough, we were ready to take the next step.

As is expected, the families met up the moment we gave them a go-ahead. This time, we were to come down to your house. So, we had flown down to Delhi together – given both our parents were put up there – and parted ways once again at airport, only to meet up the following day.

You and I had both planned to keep things simple, so it was just my parents and me who came down, unlike the whole extended family gathering that is typically called for at such an occasion. Similarly, you had made sure your parents did not go all out inviting a million relatives. Just a casual, close-family intimate thing…

I loved your mom in the very first instance. She hugged me the moment I entered the house and kissed me on the forehead. The joy of bringing home a daughter was evident in her eyes, and it put away all my fears that my friends' horror stories about their moms-in-law had built in my head. She was warm, caring and had zero expectations out of her daughter-in-law to be.

In her words, "When I do not expect anything from my own son, what right do I have to expect anything from my daughter?"

I noticed she had used the word daughter, and not daughter-in-law. I fell in love with her modern, pragmatic approach to life. We were bound to be close, I felt.

Taking back ample positive vibes, we began our six-month-long courtship. This included a million text messages each day, rushed evenings at work on weekdays to squeeze in dinners whenever possible, packed weekends to fit in wedding-shopping, partying with friends, watching movies, going to the theatre and dining out.

I recall this one weekend when I had crashed at your place after a daylong shopping spree. We dumped our belongings and flopped ourselves on the bed. By now, we had shared several kisses, clearing the initial 'stages' of love-making, as they say. But we were yet to go all the way. But that day, you had a naughty gleam in your eyes.

"Love or lust?" you asked, quizzing me after a long time.

I couldn't resist your smartass move, "Love on weekdays, lust on weekends," I said, and you laughed out loud to come on top of me to give me a demonstration of your lust.

✳ ✳ ✳

I must have passed out on the floor thinking about our days gone by, for when I opened my eyes; I saw the morning sun spread its rays on your face.

You were just about entering the house. You were in shambles. Your hair was ruffled, your shirt crumpled, your eyes red shot.

"You need to leave," you said, looking at me, and before I could react, you went into the guest bedroom and locked yourself in.

I tried to follow you into the room, but you locked it. When you did not reply even after my multiple knocks and bangs, I knew it was over. You were probably right. I should leave.

Commencement

Dearest Aarav,

I headed to our room and started to pack some of my stuff – the essentials. My initial hunch was to come to you, but somehow, it felt wrong. I needed some time alone to process everything. I wanted to be happy when I came to you, and if I went to you right now, our new start would be marked permanently, as the day I destroyed my husband's trust. So, I called up Shyna instead. Fortunately, her kid was with her folks, so she had the house to herself and was able to take me in.

Shyna was being a great friend. Very few people in this world have the ability to look at people without judging them; I must say Shyna is one of those rare souls. When I told her what had happened, she understood me perfectly well. In fact, she was glad I had mustered the courage to confess and give things a meaningful end. Not just that, looking at my state, she refused to leave me alone for more than just a few minutes.

"I messed everything up, didn't I?" I asked her, as she brought us both a glass of vodka and soda each.

"No, you took a chance at love. That's all. Rest all is collateral damage." She said it so simply; it helped put my mind instantly at ease.

"Now just try and not think about anything for a bit. There is always tomorrow to deal with everything," she comforted.

So, I stayed in all day the next day. You tried calling me, but I was not ready to speak with you, just yet. I needed more time. When you still did not give up after several calls, I texted you back saying I was okay and needed some time alone. You insisted picking me up from Shyna's place, as I might be better with you – that my place was with you now. But I had to refuse you; I was simply not in the right frame of mind to come to you yet. And so, I stayed with Shyna for a couple more days, taking some time off from office as well.

Three days later, I tried to get out. I knew I needed to do something about how things had ended with Yohan, but I was unable to find any answer sitting in that room. So, when you called again that evening, I agreed to move in with you. I thanked Shyna for everything – for being there when I was at my lowest, for not judging me, and for all the pep talk and comfort that only a friend could have provided – and packed my stuff to move in with you.

I felt my heart racing a little, as I drove to your place later that day. Just as my mind dictated my limbs to change the gear from first to third and back to first (for who can drive in the fifth in Bandra?) my heart was dictating the mind to waver my emotions between remorse and hope. Remorse over how things ended with my husband, and my urge to set the equation right in whatever little way I possibly could. I still considered him a very close one; one I had spent more than half a decade with. He deserved more than a half-ass explanation about the downturn his life had taken. But I was also hopeful. Hopeful that my moving out would probably be better for the both of us, as probably by being away from him would help reduce the hurt. Somehow, the thought of him in pain refused to leave my mind, and I knew I would not be able to come to you in full, until I knew he was alright. Until then, a part of my heart would be with him…

I know I should have been more positive about the entire thing – that it could be a new beginning for us, and we could finally be together, guilt-free. But perhaps, I took you a little for granted here. Subconsciously, my mind kept going back to him, even in moments when I should have been planning our 'happily ever after'.

It is strange that my happy memories with my husband (my *ex*-husband? No, I was not ready to call him my ex yet…) kept coming back to me, and it took some effort to bring my mind back to you. I tried consciously to think back to the reason I was here today. I brought forth your face in my mind – the way you looked at me, your smile and the touch of your fingers on my chin, just before you kissed me, the warmth of your arms.

It took some serious effort, but by the time, I entered your parking lot, and stepped out onto the patio of your building, the full-blown impact of reality just hit me. I was here; I was going to be here with you – forever. I willed myself to get into a positive frame of mind, and finally, as I stepped into the elevator, a speck of joy finally found its way to my mouth and curved it up into a smile. Our dream was finally about to come true. And I was determined to make our reality as sweet as the dream.

It was the tightest I had ever hugged you. I held you so close, as if transferring all of my emotions unto you – the joy, the pain, the hurt, the hope, the guilt, the love.

I told you the entire story about the showdown with my

husband. You were more empathetic with the situation than I had expected you to be. You nestled me in your arms and held me close through the entire recitation. Despite your efforts, the exhaustion seemed too much to handle, so we called in an early night and went off to bed, holding each other. I soaked in the feeling – this was how it would be from now on – to sleep (wishfully without any worries) in your arms.

I was finally home. Or was I?

I woke up the next day ready to start my new life with you. By now, I was used to the morning routine at your place. But it felt weird that day. I showered, while you cooked breakfast. But I missed the smell of the reed-diffused jasmine of my bathroom that day. We caught up on the morning news while eating the toast and omelette and drinking coffee, except, the conversation seemed forced that day. I then headed to arrange my stuff in the wardrobe. You had already vacated some space for me to keep my things. I stared at the empty space in front of me, and it reminded me of the emptiness constantly tugging my heart.

When I couldn't bring myself to unpack even after staring at the space for a good fifteen minutes, I just dumped the bag as is and shut the door of the wardrobe. When you left the house to get groceries, I walked around the house trying to take in the fact that this was to be my new home. However, all that I managed to assimilate was how alien it felt in there. Unable to feel anything at all despite the efforts, I simply flopped myself on the sofa, and switched on the television, forcing myself to stare at the screen. I only realized how blankly I was while looking at it, when you startled me upon your return with a vague comment on how interesting that movie was – the one I was supposedly watching.

I tried to mutter something intelligent in response, knowing all too well that you had already figured my absent-mindedness and were just testing me to see how long I could go on putting up a show of being alright. You decided to play along and quizzed me on the previous scene, and I made an excuse that I had just got off a call with Shyna – the reason I could not catch it. When I refused to give up the pretense, you tried to make me talk about my uneasiness, but I held it back from you – not wanting to bring up the topic of my husband on our first official day together. You tried multiple times to lighten up my mood, albeit, I was unable to get over my mulling despite your efforts to snap me out of it, though I did continue to act interested in everything (but of course, you knew me all too well to believe my fake laughs and false enthusiasm). You planned on going out for lunch – which I refused politely. You suggested ordering in, and I instinctively asked you to call for *Pav Bhaji*, realizing only too late how it had been Yo and my favourite order-in food. At last, when the conversation continued to remain awkward despite your efforts, you surrendered and let me have my timeout.

I must have zombied around for a couple of days more, before finally accepting things for what they were, how they were. In those two days, you did not once rub in my face the drastic change we had just undergone (although, I fail to fathom how you managed it, since you very well deserved a happy beginning with me instead of this sulking woman living, eating and sleeping in your apartment!). You were there by my side like you always had been, but also gave me my space to recoup on my own, at my pace.

On day three, I finally awoke with a different energy. I decided I needed to do something to snap myself out of this zombie-zone. I decided to start by making the space homelier. So as a first step, I made you leave the house, promising a surprise upon your return. You were more than happy to oblige looking at my pepped-up energy after so long. Now, back at work I first printed a picture of the two of us together in Goa, found a wall-frame with a boring picture to have it replaced with ours, and hung it up on the bedroom wall. Next, I looked up a nursery nearby and called for some home plants – placing a couple of big ones in the living room and the small ones on the kitchen window-sill and added one on the dining table as well. I added some pillows and a throw on the sofa, changed the linen to a brighter shade and arranged my clothes in the wardrobe. At last, I cooked us both a full meal of *roti, sabzi, daal* and rice. Now, this was home.

I called you back home once everything was ready. You were so pleasantly surprised at the makeover.

Your first reaction was to hug me, and next was to tease me, "Thank God you did not touch my gadgets! They are a no-go zone." I hit you laughingly and apologized for my behaviour for the previous two days.

"I am so glad to have you back, my silly Anya!"

And that was how we returned to normalcy. For a while at least.

Closure

Dearest Yohan,

It was Monday, but even the ton loads of work gave me no respite from the fatigue I felt from the heavy emotional outflow from the previous few days. A lot had occurred over the past couple of weeks, a lot needed to be still figured out.

To begin with, there was the matter of settling in with *him*. It had been ten days since I had moved in with him (and two weeks since I had moved out from our home – yes, I was keeping a count), but everything still seemed so different. At first, I was completely lost. Then I tried to spruce things up and take charge myself. I started putting in effort in making the place homelier.

We were still in the process of actually getting used to being together, to start believing in our forever. It felt different to be with *him* and not think of going back home (yes, I still thought of *our* house as my home. Though, to be honest, I did make a mental note to think of a way to address that. Perhaps, a move to a new home might help? The more I thought of it, the more I believed that we, you included, needed a fresh start – a little distancing from all the chaos surrounding us). It felt different to wake up to perfection every day – yes, he was completely opposite to you in matters of cleanliness; while you were a messy man who would struggle to find your socks, he had a borderline OCD and preferred to have everything in order at all times. I had made space for myself in his closet, but I missed the familiarity of my customized cupboards. Most of all, I missed my old reading corner. Remember how we had put in great effort in designing a mini-library in a section of our house that flaunted our joint collection of the hundred plus books that we had collected over the years? And the uber cozy chaise lounge in that section that we had spent a bomb on, with an over-hanging reading lamp – it was just perfect for a good night's read after a tiring day. Unfortunately, he lacked passion for reading, so I was making do with reading on his leather recliner chair for now (no complaints from my always-tired body on this front). On the other hand, his collection of scale cars that took up a significant portion of the showcase on his drawing room wall was quite unsettling to my eyes. But like a typical fan-boy that he is, he had sworn me to not fidget it, and so, I was going to need to put in effort in getting used to it.

More importantly, it felt different to not wake up to you every morning. It felt different to not rush about the house picking up stuff you had forgotten to keep away from the previous night, to not plan meals and discuss splitting chores with you. It felt different to not annoy you with my many demands and it felt different to not even pick silly fights with you. Yes, it all felt very different, and in some corner of my heart, it felt odd. In some corner of my heart, it felt wrong.

And it was wrong, even to *him*. After all, here I was, with the man I always dreamt to be with, and for some unknown reason, all I could make myself think of was you.

I had tried calling you several times every day since the day I moved out, even texting. It had become a sort of a ritual to try your number multiple times a day – upon waking up, before leaving for office, at lunch break, before starting my car to get back from office, before crashing in for the night – and then after a no-response on all occasions, to leave you text messages. Unfortunately, it was all to no avail. You had shut me out completely. Having run out of all options, I had asked your friend – Sushant – to check in on you. I had briefly explained to him that we had a rift, causing me to move out, and that you were not answering my calls ever since. The news from him was not encouraging. He had gone to our house immediately after my call, and found you to be in more or less the same state I had left you in. The house was a mess, as were you. Moreover, in turn, you clearly asked Sushant to ask me to stop bothering you. Knowing this upset me even more, for there was nothing more I wanted than to separate on good terms, after all, I still did see you as a very dear, close friend. You deserved an explanation, to say the least. And a closure. But from the way things stood, it seemed you would be taking a long time to heal from the wounds you had suffered.

Finally, one day when I could take it no more, I decided to barge in on you. I still had the house keys, so I just let myself in one evening. I had also thought of the excuse I would use – that I wanted to collect some of my stuff. So, I waited and waited until you returned.

When you got home, I was both shocked and thrilled to see you. Thrilled because of the joy I felt upon seeing you after so long (which made me realize that this was the longest we had stayed apart ever since we got married), and shocked because of the state you were in. While you were still impeccably dressed, you had swapped your light stubble for a full-grown, unkempt beard. It did suit you, though. However, it seemed moisture had found a permanent place in your heart and extracted all life out of them. It pierced my heart to see you so disheartened. I was going to fix that right, I determined.

You almost took a step back when you saw me seated inside. I was sure I saw you contemplate leaving the house again, before you chose to finally enter. You almost ignored me thereafter, trying to walk straight to the bedroom, but I stopped you in your track.

"You will need to listen to me, Yo, please," I told you, holding your hand in a tone that was half-pleading, half-commanding. You did not say anything, but you did not move away either. So, I took my opportunity.

"Yo, I want to just explain myself to you once. Please sit down so I can talk to you." You still did not move, but turned around and said to me, "Anya, I do not want to listen to any of your sob stories. Just leave me alone."

"No Yohan, please don't run away like this. I know I did wrong, and I am sorry for it. All I am asking for is to give me one chance to explain to you, to vent my heart's apology to you. I really do care for you, Yo, and I cannot stand to leave you like this. We had such a good story – you and I – we cannot end it like this. It will not be a fair end to us. And I will never be able to forgive myself if I am unable to convince you to not shut me out like this. I really, really want to give us an amicable closure. Please just listen to me once?" I was literally begging you to give me that one chance to redemption.

But alas, when you did speak up, I found no hope in your words, "You already gave us a closure the day you chose to see him again. But what surprises me is that we did indeed have a good story. Unfortunately, you never seemed to have believed in it, only having stuck in your past always. If anything, *you* needed a closure with your guy before you started your story with me, Anya.

"And, if you still really want to do anything for me, then just stay away from me. Just remove yourself from my life, forever. I do not ever want to see you or hear you again."

With that, you removed my hand off your arm and walked away into the room. You just turned one last time to say, "I am not sure whether you have informed your family about this, but just so you know, I let mine know about it yesterday. They will get in touch with your parents to sort out whatever needs to be sorted out – legally, formally, whatever. And yes, next time, it will be better if you can send someone else over to collect your stuff."

You shut the door in my face once again.

I stood there numbly; lost of any last hope I had had before coming into the house. I knew the guilt of what I had done was going to haunt me forever, and I would never be able to forgive myself for how things ended between us. But most of all, I tried to fathom the truth in your words. Maybe it was time to indeed remove myself from your life. When I left our house that day, I left my set of keys on the table.

Transition

Dearest Aarav,

A few more days passed by in a haze. My parents had found out from my husband's parents about what had happened between us. It could not have been more embarrassing for them, but even though I knew this would happen, I had not gathered courage to speak with them myself. They were on the verge of disowning me. It was all getting too much to handle. I wish I had managed the situation better, but I was so consumed by the thought of simply pacifying my husband, that all else seemed secondary. I know it sounds crude to have ignored my parents like that, but I knew them well, and I knew it would be easier to handle them if I went to them after I had at least salvaged some of the damage caused.

The only bright side amongst everything was that we were adjusting better in our lives together. Yet, the constant lump of guilt I was living with was starting to affect everything I did. Unconsciously, I was bringing up the mention of my husband in all our conversations. I kept trying to devise ways to pacify him. You were being very understanding, but even in my half-dazed state I could see your patience was being tested. I knew I had to get a hold of matters before I messed everything up once again.

Hoping a cup of coffee might help put my mind at ease, I headed to the breakout area of my office. I was still submerged in my thoughts at the vending machine when Animesh, the VP, walked over. He was dressed sharply as always – a semi-formal blazer that suited his well-built, tall frame well and also reflected his superiority over others in the firm. Unlike all other times when I had had to initiate small talk, this time, he started the conversation. Little did I know that what he was about to say was going to change my life forever.

"Ms. Dynamite! Good to bump into you," he said, placing his cup under the outlet of the vending machine, as I pulled mine out. "I was about to call you for a small chat myself. Can we catch up for a bit after you are done with your coffee?"

"Sure," I replied, and saw him walk away purposefully with his steaming latte in hand, greeting some of the other senior folks along the way.

Ten minutes later, I was in his cabin for the 'chat'. Typical of any discussion, he started with context.

"By the way, that was a superb performance on the Dew account. My congratulations!"

"Thanks, Animesh. But you know it was a team effort."

"Being modest now, are we? he tried to joke.

"Anyhow, tell me this," he continued, a little more seriously now, "How does the idea of heading the Dew account from the city of their headquarters sound to you?"

"Headquarters? Aren't they based out of London?"

"That's right. If you are up for it, I would like to initiate the process to send you over to our London branch. After all, Dew is a global account, and having you there will help ensure seamless transitioning."

I could not believe what he had just said. I could not go to London. My life was here, you were here. And what about my husband? How would he react if he found out I was considering moving to London?

Although, come to think of it, I was sure the move to London would not really affect my husband. Particularly so, now that he knew about us. His angst had rendered me dead to him in any case. Therefore, London or Lisbon was not going to make a difference…

Animesh must have guessed my shock from the blank look on my face. Maybe that's why he was quick to add, "Take your time to think about it, no pressure. When you are ready, we could talk about your role there. I am trying to convince the leadership to move you up into the position of Director. It can be a great jump for you. I am confident you will be able to do well there."

The promotion, after all! My mind started racing at the impact this could have on all our lives. Perhaps, this move could be the answer to everything, after all…

"I'm ready to move," I said, almost too instantly.

"Are you sure?" he was a little taken aback by the suddenness of my reply, "Don't you want to discuss with your husband first? We have time until this weekend, in case you want to think it through…"

The husband, right…

"That won't be necessary. I am sure I want to move. Thank you so much for making this happen."

"Alright then, let me loop you in on the conversations I have been having with our folks there. Kane, as you know, my counterpart in London, is leading this transition, and he will put you in touch with their HR, who can work out the offer and guide you on the formalities, visa – the works."

"Great! I look forward to it. Thanks once again."

As I stepped out of his cabin, I realized I had taken an irreversible decision that was going to affect all our lives. I could only hope it was for the better.

The rest of the day passed by in a haze. I was quickly pulled into calls and discussions around the move. More processes were lined up for the following few days. The plan was to get the internal formalities sorted that week so the visa could be sent for processing by the start of the next week. They were optimistic that as long as something unexpected did not pop up, I would be able to move within the next six weeks. I had not expected things to move so quickly, but they did! By the end of it, I was positive I had made the right decision.

On my way back to your place that evening, I pondered over my decision. I was hopeful that moving away would help my husband heal better. It would help me be at peace too, knowing that I was giving him the full space he would need to get over me, and by taking away any chance encounters that were likely to bring him even more pain.

As relief started setting in, my thoughts drifted towards a happier place. This happy place we would be calling ours. I imagined our life together in the new city. A quaint little house with eclectic interiors, a dog – a pug – running about our living room, scratching its way up onto our sofa, where we were sitting cuddling each other, sipping on some wine, watching Notting Hill on the television…

Finally, there was excitement. I could not wait to tell you about the move to London.

When I reached home (our home?), you were already in. For some reason, you seemed chirpier than usual. There was clearly something brewing that you were dying to tell me.

"What is it? Is there some good news that hasn't reached me yet?" I teased, sharing your joy.

"You know me so well! Here's what happened…" you bought out what you had been hiding until now behind.

It was a trophy! "You were awarded! Wow, congratulations!" I came over to you and hugged you.

"Tell me all about it," I urged.

"Well, what can I say? The month-long separation from you paid off. This is the recognition from the CEO that I received for expanding our brand in the Asia-Pacific region. If all goes well, I should be promoted by the end of the year!"

"Wow! That is awesome. You truly deserve it…" and I genuinely was, except for the slight concern your last statement had raised.

"What? Something off?" you read me correctly.

"No, nothing at all! This calls for a celebration. What should we do?"

"You don't need to worry about it. I have already ordered in."

"Great! So, while we are celebrating, I too have some good news to share."

"Is that so? Go ahead, shoot!"

"So, you remember how I was dragged into the Dew Beverages account – the endless nights, the crazy discussions, the needless revisions…"

"Yeah, of course. What about it? Did they expand the contract with you guys?"

"Yes, that they did. But that's not what I am excited about."

"Then what is it?"

"Well, I too got plenty of accolades for my dedication on the project. So much so that they are willing to put me on the global team for the account, that's in London, with a possible move to the Director position."

"Woah, now that indeed is something! Surely this calls for a double celebration." You were genuinely happy, and I wondered if you had heard the entire news carefully.

"Thanks!"

You moved on to the dining table to unscrew the bottle of the expensive sparkling white wine you seemed to have purchased for the occasion.

"Umm, Aarav…" I probed, just to be sure, "The position will be in London."

"Yeah, I figured that. But surely, even if you don't move to London you can still be a Director here. Isn't that what you had planned on, anyways?" You said this as if London was never even part of the offering.

"Before I got the offer, yes. But don't you see this is just too good to refuse. You will come with me to London, won't you?" I probed with my heart in my mouth, for I could not read your reaction from where you stood.

"What? Why should I need to move to London?" you asked, genuinely not seeing your role in the entire scenario.

"Because I will be moving there…?" I stated obviously.

"Are you kidding me? I can't move to London right now! I

am aiming at heading the Asia Pacific region by next year. So, obviously I need to stay in the region. Moving to London would mean giving up on that and starting afresh. You can't be expecting that of me," you said, half laughing, as if it was a silly proposition.

"But then, what about my promotion?"

"Oh, come on Anya. You can always take the promotion here, without actually moving to London."

"But that is where their global headquarters is. I can't manage the Dew account from here…"

"Oho, don't stress about it. You can take up some other account here. I know it won't be that big, but it is okay to compromise sometimes. I will make up for both our success. Come now, I'm sure you will find a way to convince them. You are good at convincing people," you winked.

"I'm sorry, what?" I tried to digest what you had just said, but it was too shocking to accept, "You cannot possibly make up for both our successes – from here *or* from anywhere. How can you, of all people, even think of something like that? How would you like it if I said the same for you – come with me Aarav, I will make up for both our successes in London!" I snapped back.

"You are making a big deal out of it."

"And you keep saying the same for every big issue that pops up between us. You know what, Aarav? I had thought you will take it a little better this time around," I was getting worked up now.

"I *am* taking it well enough. Why do you think I am popping open this wine?" You noticed I was clearly angry now, but still chose to downplay it.

"By better I meant I had thought you would be more willing to come with me to London."

"You know that is not possible for me, Anya," you said plainly, still uncorking the wine.

"Why not? Did I not leave everything and come to you – my husband, my house, my family! And you cannot leave even a city for me? You cannot even think of giving it a shot?"

"I will. In a couple of years, okay? Now is just not the right time. Listen, I know you have gone through a big unsettlement, but is it necessary that I also undergo a similar transformation in order to prove my love to you?"

I pondered over your arguments and, if I am being honest, you did have a point. Yet, neither was my mind ready to give up on the offer I was being made nor did my heart have the strength to let go of this chance of the three of us (my husband included) making a fresh start that we all needed.

When I did not say anything, you persisted, coming over to me and holding me by the waist, "Listen. We will figure something out. Worst case, we do long distance."

The word long distance sent another round of shivers down my spine. The pain from several years ago came rushing back. We could not let ourselves through it once again. We could not take the chance of history repeating itself.

"Anya, I know it sounds scary. But trust me, it will be okay. So what if it did not work out last time? We have both matured up now. And we are strong. We will manage. Believe me."

Are we that strong? I found me questioning.

You hugged me lightly, and then proceeded to get the glasses that were now filled. "Come, let's not spoil our mood now, this is a moment to be happy, not gloomy," you said, raising a toast to us. The bubbly sparkled in the flute as I joined you in the celebration, pushing aside my musing for later in the day, when I knew I would be lying awake in my bed – something else that seemed very normal nowadays.

We toasted to our new successes, as we sipped on our wine and slow danced to the tunes of Eric Clapton's Wonderful Tonight. We moved on to the dining table, where the garlic prawns and the grilled fish waited invitingly. You elaborated your exact plans for the promotion, oblivious to the wet gleam that had gathered in corner of my eyes.

Transformation

Dearest Aarav,

I tried to bury the topic of London under the bush, and tried to convince myself that I was indeed making a mountain of a mole hill and we will figure out something in the end. We had not come all this way to give up over this one disagreement, had we? I also considered making the compromise myself and staying back, dropping the plan of London – after all, letting you go was not an option I had considered in the wildest of my dreams. The other factor probing me to stay back was that I did not want any more regrets in life for not trying my best. I had let you go once and suffered for a very long time. I had let go of my husband and I was still suffering. I could not think of letting go of you again, it was not an option.

And so, I tried to move on. I focused on making things work. This time, I put my heart and soul into it – as did you. We started living like the couple we had always dreamt to be. I genuinely tried my best to silence the voice in my head that screamed 'guilty' every time I got into a silly laugh or a mushy blush. I won't say I was a hundred percent successful at removing the thought of my husband from my head, but I tried a hundred percent to make you happy, to make our lives together happy.

I would cook you a meal on my lighter days or surprise you with a naughty number on an odd night here and there. I continued adding knick-knacks of curios to our house to make it cozier; and enjoyed teasing you on your silly boy-toy collection. We had lovely days – evening walks, weekend movies, Sunday brunches and a lot of sex. As a matter of fact, I cannot recall having a single argument – big or small – in the course of those few weeks. If I look back to it now, those were happy times for us.

You too tried your bit to try and pacify me, for you did realize how difficult it would have been for you to make a similar sacrifice yourself. You even offered to check with your firm if you could take the position in London yourself. But I knew you did not mean to actually take that up with a whole heart, so I did not let you go about it (yes, Aarav, you might be ruthless in pursuing your goals, but I respected you for your drive and was not going to stop you from chasing them for my needs). In consolation, you promised me a lovely life with you here, in our home in Mumbai, and you were right in that there would be nothing lacking if I stayed back. You tried to create some special moments, so I could appreciate what we had here – loving me, pampering me and protecting me. And I would be lying if I said I did not see what I had at stake – I loved you way too much to stand even the thought of living without you.

Eventually, I decided to give up the position at London. I planned on letting Animesh know as soon as I got an opportunity to speak with him in person. However, something happened in the interim that made me question my decision…

✸ ✸ ✸

A month had passed by uneventfully since the last disagreement, and the holiday season of Christmas was upon us. This time, your office had arranged its annual gala dinner for its employees at the Taj Lands End, closer to the holidays, and families and partners were invited. I had assumed conveniently that we would both be attending it as a couple – formally, finally. However, it surprised me when you announced that we weren't yet at the stage where we could call ourselves *official*!

"Are you serious!" I remember being shocked at your comment. "So, do I need to marry you now to be your official plus one?"

We had not really talked about 'marriage' as yet, and so the topic was fresh territory for the both of us here.

"Well, we *will* marry someday, right?" you replied, and I won't deny feeling slightly happy seeing you have the thought of our marriage at the back of your mind.

"Well, I do hope so! But what until then?" I retorted regardless, a little too quickly, a little too up-handedly.

"Until then we need to be cautious about how we present ourselves in the corporate environment, that's all," you replied.

"Says Mr Aarav Mehra, who was only too keen to have me take advantage of our so called *'situation'* when it came to my corporate environment," I scoffed.

"That was different. You stood to gain something out of it. Here, that is not the case."

But of course, you could not see me upset for long, so you relented.

"Alright, if it makes you happy, we will go together."

I grinned broadly, elated that we would finally be making a public appearance together as a couple, and embraced you in a happy hug.

***

On the day of the event, I put in good time to get dressed. I chose a lime green georgette gown that was highlighted my form nicely, albeit in a classy sort of way. I visited the salon to do my perms and wore my hair down, so they flirted with my neckline just perfectly. The light-yellow eye-shadow and pink lipstick finished the look. Satisfied with my appearance, I glanced at you to see you perfectly groomed in a blue blazer with a black, round-neck t-shirt, khakis and matching loafers. I made you pose for a selfie and was pleased at how good we looked together as a couple.

The party was wonderful, and it was evident that your firm had spared no expense in making it lavish. Alcohol of all brands circulated freely, along with the choicest spread of appetizers. We headed to the bar to get a drink, where I encountered the first dampener of the evening.

Just as you ordered a dry martini for me, your colleague Vinay walked up to us, giving you a pat on the back as a greeting. He was holding his whiskey and seemed to have been on his third already, I supposed. When he asked about me, you casually introduced me as 'your friend from college, whom you caught up with recently'.

I was surprised as to why would you hide our status to your office folks, and probed you about it, but you downplayed it saying he was not important enough to know the details.

I let this incident go by, until we were in a group of your core team – your brand's country head Siddhant, the senior marketing guy Anirudh and your Asia Pacific category head – the boss lady, who was pushing for your promotion to as the Asia Pacific brand head – Lilian Oh (who had travelled down from Hong Kong that week and had stayed back specially to attend the party). As they exchanged pleasantries and introduced their respective better halves, I was caught off-guard when you once again chose to simply address me as a casual friend, "She is Anya, an old friend of mine that I recently caught up with, here in Mumbai."

I questioned you on it once we broke from the group, only to be told, "Let's talk about it later, please."

Of course, the fact that you were not ready to open-up about us did not go down well with me. I spent an uneasy time thereafter, as you left me at the lounge sofa to go and catch up with the rest of your office mates. I was still pondering about your behaviour, when I noticed something that set me further at unrest.

You were in a circle of about five to six people, along with Siddhant and Lilian, raising a toast to one of the guys. The next thing I see is Lilian put her hand on your shoulder, and whisper something in your ear. I saw you laugh back and put your hand on the small of her waist, excusing yourselves from the group to lead her to the side of the room for a chat that seemed a little too friendly to me.

Now, I am not one to suspect you of flirting unnecessarily with other women. However, I am not naïve enough to not know to differentiate a casual chat from something more. I downed my drink as I walked up to you, trying to claim my man back from her. You figured how I had intruded and glared at me the moment Lilian had excused herself. The rest of the evening I tried to mingle with your friends, but you seemed distracted by Lilian and tried finding ways to get a one-on-one time with her again – which you did eventually towards the latter part of the evening, and I had to look away when I saw you guys hit it off once again in a similar fashion as before!

Once back in the car, I was unable to hold back and wanted nothing more than confront you right away. Somehow, you beat me to it.

"What did you just do? Do you realize how important she is for my move to the Asia Pacific head?" you accused me, as you put the car into gear.

I was annoyed that you would try to pin this back on me, "What did *I* do? You were the one flirting with her! And not to mention you did not even introduce me properly to even a single one of your colleagues!"

"Oh Anya, please don't start this again. Firstly, I did tell you that we need to be cautious about our relationship in the formal circle. Secondly, it was just a chat. And if anything, *she* was the one trying to hit on me, not the other way around."

"And you were only too happy to let her," I snubbed.

"Look, she is the most important person in my career at this point in time. So, if keeping her happy requires me to get a little friendly with her, I will do exactly that. I do not want you and your old-school attitude to judge me for that," you said, as you hit the brake at the signal, "You should trust me enough by now to know it is nothing more than that."

I found it difficult to digest that you saw *nothing* wrong here.

"Are you implying that you will '*flirt*' with your boss to get that promotion?"

"I don't see any harm in being a little casual. Didn't I tell you the same when it was about *our* relationship for *your* contract with our firm?"

"And I had not been comfortable with it even back then."

"You should not have been uncomfortable even back then. These things are quite common now," you tried to calm down, as you drove and hit the gear once again at the blink of the green light.

"Oh please, don't give me this crap about cozying up to your boss to appease her for your promotion being '*common*'!" I was nowhere close to being calm.

"Well, it is true," you laid your left hand on mine as you added, "Plus, the most important thing is to trust each other on these matters. Me getting friendly with her is not going to affect our relationship. It is you I love, not her. A little bit of casual flirting is not going to change that, Anya."

You put it so causally, it made me wonder if it was only too commonplace for you to act like this. Were you like this all along, or was this something new? Surely, the old Aarav had never eyed another woman in all the time we were together.

Once again, it made me question whether the Aarav I was with now was the Aarav I had been in love with or was it just the idea of him I was holding on to. I needed to find out, and so I nudged you further.

"If you do love me as you say you do, you should be in a position to give me the respect that a loved one deserves – not shy away from introducing her to your friends and colleagues."

"I did introduce you."

"But not as your girlfriend."

"There you go making a big deal out of nothing once again."

"What do you mean by 'once again'?"

You gave me a look and said, "You know as well as I do that you have a habit of over-thinking and over-reacting. You have been doing it for almost all matters of late!"

"Oh really! Is that what you have been thinking of me? I have been trying hard to adapt to the changes, as well as accept all your decisions, and all I get in return is that I over-react. Wonderful!"

You looked at me quietly before saying what you said next, but when you did, you did not meet my eye.

You said, "On the contrary, I have been the one who has been amply supportive of your long face over the past couple of weeks. Don't think I have not noticed how you keep bringing up your *ex-husband* up in every conversation we have been having. It is high time I get shown some support in return now.

"And let us not pretend that you sacrificed and adapted everything for me. You know it as well as I do that you were already fed up of your marriage *before* I came into your life this time. I was just an easy escape for you from your already broken marriage."

I stood shell shocked for a moment. Your words had stung me like a bee's sting. I was dumbstruck by what you had just said. How could you be so harsh? On one hand you had been sweeter than I had ever expected you to be in the last few days, but on the other hand, you just washed all that off by uttering the words you just did.

Yet, deny it as I might, I had to admit it was the truth, one that I had known all along, but would not allow even my subconscious to accept. The truth was that I was not only '*not*' seeking marriage, but that I was in fact running *away* from it.

Still, that did not change the fact that I had left everything for you. The thoughts and the doubts I had pushed aside on many nights in the past few months came rushing back to me. I was once again facing the ever-pragmatic Aarav. The one who never compromised with his plans but expected me to follow him with all the sacrifices. The compromises and sacrifices had always been one-sided. This was how it had been in the past, and I realized now, that if we were to be together, then this is how it will be in the future, too. Was I ready to accept it?

We stopped at the parking lot of your building, and you turned to me as you turned the ignition off. "I am sorry, that was a little too harsh."

I did not reply to you, and we made our way up to your apartment. You kissed me as we entered in, but I turned away from you, the question still looming in my head, and walked up to the balcony overlooking the towering buildings flickering away the lights through their tiny windows, illuminating the otherwise dark, gloomy night. The rain shattered on the tree leaves just like the shattering of my illusion of a blooming romance. This relationship – which I was using as my escape from a mundane marriage. Not that I was feeling guilty, but the realization, followed by the admittance was surely making what we had between us seem smaller than 'love'.

You apologized again, kissing me as a way to make-up. And I let you. On the surface, everything seemed perfect. Except, today your kiss didn't send a spark running down my spine, today, your gaze did not make me melt, today, your arms did not feel like home. Today, you started to seem like a stranger, once again.

FAREWELL

Dearest Aarav,

Hard as I tried to put the event being me, the reality of our relationship started haunting me. The reality that staying back was not going to take away one of the core problems of our relationship – the fact that the Aarav I was with today was a different person from the Aarav I had loved over eight years ago. Or perhaps, you had been the same all along, only I was seeing you differently now? For you see, Aarav, people can change their behaviour, but not their nature, their instinct. And it was your instinct to pursue what you desired, particularly professionally. You were never going to act contrary to this nature of yours. Now, don't take me wrong, I did not expect you to shed your dreams for me at the drop of a hat. But I did expect you to be respectful of our relationship when chasing them. To be flexible enough to accommodate my dreams as well in yours. I did not expect you to put a ring on my finger in an impulse. But I did expect you to give me the respect of a loved one that I deserved, that I showered on you wholeheartedly.

Therefore, if I were to choose to stay, I had to be prepared to accept this fact about you. The problem was I was not sure if I was okay accepting this imbalance.

Thus, with each passing day, the feeling of aloofness grew in me; the desire to get away grew stronger. Instinctively, I carried on with the visa processes, hoping that by the time the final day arrived, I would have the answers to all my uncertainties. I know I blind-sided you in this and should have felt guilty. But when in the following month you again left for one of your month-long conferences, it became easier to keep the fact from you, and I convinced myself that not telling something was not technically lying...

As the day of decision drew closer, I knew a few difficult choices lay in front of me. These choices were to define the future course of our lives. It was not going to be easy. And yet, it had to be done.

On one hand was you and our undying love – love that had endured years of trials and tests. And the reality that staying apart had left me lost in life, going with the flow, without really living it. The pain that I suffered several years ago still felt so fresh that I shuddered at the mere thought of reliving it. I simply did not have it in me to bear it again.

On the other hand, was the shattering dream of the life I had envisioned to live with you. I never dreamt of making it big, but I did dream of being successful. I never willed myself into making sacrifices for my work, but I gave it my heart and soul. I never expected you to give up your dreams for me, but I did not want to tread that path myself, either. Especially not if they seemed to be trivial to you. And most importantly, I never asked a hundred promises of you, but I did expect a hundred percent you from you – mind, body and soul.

✳ ✳ ✳

The day of my scheduled meeting with Animesh arrived – the one which I had planned to let him know of my decision to call off my move to London. I realized that if I called it off now, I may not get the opportunity again. As I stood there trying to make a final choice, my mind wandered back to the times I spent with you. Inadvertently, memories of my husband whom I hurt to be with you were interwoven, too. Flashes of our times together, and of those with my husband, appear in front of me as I close my eyes – like two movies running in parallel in fast forward. Flashes of time I met you for the first time at that party and of the first time I met my husband at the café. Flashes of my first kiss ever that I shared with you on that night by the sea and those of the honeymoon to Seychelles with my husband. Of the many nights you and I spent talking endlessly, secretly. And of the numerous parties my husband and I hosted as a perfect team. And of course, flashes of our separation eight years ago and the seemingly endless torment that followed, as well as of the horrible arguments that I had with my husband over the years of our marriage. Then, last, flashes of our reunion last year and my reunion with my husband, a month ago that night at Santorini.

As I stood there weighing the preciousness of these moments, they shed their feather-light nostalgia, and instead gained the burden of a guilt-ridden life. A life I spent in search of love and spent in losing much more than love.

When I thought of it like this, the choice seemed so simple. The choice was a life where I was wanted and loved wholly at all times, not one where a part of me (or my choice) was a secondary priority. The choice was a place where I could flourish fearlessly, not one where my dreams were termed frivolous.

Yes, Aarav. I knew this was going to come as a shock to you, but I had understood that some roads in life must be treaded alone. I took a long time in understanding this, and hurt more than a few people along the way, but I had learned that happiness cannot be defined by how others treat you, but by how you treat yourself. That is exactly what I had decided – to treat myself with dignity and love. I had decided, Aarav that I would be moving to London – with or without you.

***

You respected my decision when I broke the news to you, having half expected it. You did not question me on my choice even once. But you could not hide the slight tear that rolled down the corner of your eye when you held me after that.

You said a million sweet things to me that day, and over the course of the remaining days we had together. Yet, a zillion words remain unsaid.

I too cried in your arms a hundred times about how I was going to miss you. Yet, a thousand tears were left un-cried.

We made promises about how we were going to make it work long-distance this time. Yet, a lifetime of promises remained unfulfilled.

You and I both knew that we were leaving matters in the hands of fate once again, fate that we did not trust, despite our modern, pragmatic selves.

Perhaps, in a way it was better that you were leaving before me, for we could not have endured the sullenness for more days than we did (was it ten odd days from when I had announced my decision to you?). This time, when I dropped you at the airport for your two-week conference, you promised to book a ticket to London soon and see me before long. We held each other for what seemed like eternities, but when we parted, we knew in the heart of our hearts that when we would be meeting again, we would be different people.

As I bid you goodbye, I hoped we would have the opportunity to love each other again in this lifetime. But should destiny deny us this gratification, I would like to let you know that I loved you with every cell of my blood – not once, but twice. Every moment spent with you; I was completely yours.

HOPE

Dearest Yohan,

I do not know if there could have been any better way to handle is. When you stopped taking my calls and refused to speak let alone see me, I was enveloped by this blanket of guilt a permanent lump in my throat. No matter where I went d, your vision from that black-night kept haunting me.

that day had said so much more than just hate furious look in your eyes screamed aloud the u tried to hide beneath your angst. But my each one of them. I knew you were more rtbroken than sad, and more destroyed

way I had not expected. It was not though I was prepared to be something different. Your ng.

at work, at home, while driving,

while eating – the lump in my throat kept growing, hoping for you to give me one sign to show you hadn't closed yourself on me. My concern for you grew with each passing day, as I knew you were like me, and if I had chosen to not vent my wrath out on the person responsible for hurting me in the way that I had hurt you, I would be drowning in my own despair.

I realized I needed to do whatever it took to find you your peace again, although I knew it was not going to be easy.

So, when the opportunity to distance myself from you presented itself to me, I did not hesitate to take it up. I thought this was possibly for the best – the farther I would be from you, the easier it would be to cope for you. I was trying my best to remove myself completely from your life, so that my memories do not upset you anymore.

This was what I texted you that day, hoping against hope that you had not blocked me:

Just writing to say I thought about what you said the other day. Will try and stay away so you can have your space and hopefull heal from the hurt I caused you. Wishing you the best for li Hope you can forgive me someday…

P.S. I am moving to London by the end of the m Permanently this time.

I hit send before I could change my mind, wishing we ourselves some avenue to remain friends, for I did truly s my close one. However, I respected your decision to nc wished you the best in life, always.

With that in mind, I accepted my defeat in pa had given up all hope of seeing you ever again, fo remained before my flight to London. Howeve incomplete, and in the heart of my hearts, I kne more…

I was proven right when I stepped out of the office that Friday. I entered the parking lot, looking for my car (my horrible habit of forgetting my spot every single time), when I spotted you next to it.

I squinted to make sure it was really you. It indeed was, and I cried as I rushed to you.

"Yo!" was all I could muster as I walked up to you, stopping a couple of steps from you, unsure if hugging you will offend you and make you leave again.

"I knew I would find you here," you said simply.

"I can't believe I am finally seeing you."

"Me neither. To be honest, I don't know if I am still over it, or if I can ever be. But then, no matter how hard I tried, I could not avoid you any longer."

"No, Yo. You have the right to be very, very mad at me. I deserve it all," I was on the verge of tears.

"Let us go somewhere and talk?" you offered, noticing the teardrop that had gathered on the corner of my eye.

We got into the car and drove quietly to the nearest café – not bothering which one it was or what it served. When I had adjusted my seat so I could face you easily, I began with the monologue I had rehearsed in my head so many times in the hope of seeing you again. But words betrayed me when the time came. All I could do was hold you and cry my heart out.

"It's alright, Anya," you held me by my shoulders so I could face you. You looked me in the eye and started, part matter-of-factly, part caringly.

"What is done is done. I have given it a lot of thought, undergone the mourning that I needed to and let out all the anger I had in me. I am now ready to deal with matters practically and see them for what they really are.

"Anya, I know you really love that guy. He is the one you had told me about the first day we met – isn't he? Well, that bastard is one lucky guy."

I smiled for the first time that day. You continued then, "I do still blame you for having blind-sided me the way you did. But again, if I put myself in your shoes (although you know I would never ever be in your shoes in this case), I don't know what other way there could have been to handle the situation. So, I have decided to let you know that I hold no grudge. After all, deny as I might, you still do hold a very special place in my heart. And always will. But I will try my best to move on, I will just have to learn how to. Which is why I need to distance myself from you – if you know what I mean."

"I do, Yo. And you are just as special to me too. I can't thank you enough for coming here today. Believe me, I was ready to go through hell to save you the grief I gave you. And I want nothing more than for you to be happy. I get it that I need to give you your space to move on. So, you will be happy to know that I have taken up the offer to move to London and will be out of your way Yo. But, remember this – I will be there for you whenever you need me," I promised.

"Oh yes, London…now that is big! Congratulations! I always knew you would make it." You spoke easily, but I knew it was still difficult for you.

"Thanks," I muttered, realizing that this could be the last time we were seeing each other.

"So, when are you guys flying out?" you asked, awkwardly.

"Uh, well, it is just me for now. I will be leaving the day after."

"Day after! That is soon. But why alone? What about your guy – he is joining you after, is he?"

I felt awkward in letting you know the truth. "I don't know. It's…not that simple. He is due for a promotion and doing really well for himself here, so…maybe he won't join me in London."

"Are you kidding me! Is he mad or what? Somebody needs to put some sense into this idiot. I hope he realizes what he is letting go of…" despite everything, I melted at the fact that you were still concerned for me.

"Thanks. I hope he comes around."

"If it were me, I would never have let you leave alone, Anya, I would have decided to come with you in the blink of an eye," you said, holding my gaze this time. I could still see the pain in your eyes, and they only made me feel embarrassed even more.

"I wish I had never let you go, Yo," the words slipped out of my mouth before I could stop them.

"And I wish we could just reverse the time back to where we had begun."

"Then we wouldn't be where we are. So many things I would have done differently…"

I was left mid-sentence when the waiter walked up to us, asking for our order, breaking us from our moment.

"Anyhow, I must get going," you said. Awkwardly, sprucing yourself back to your cordial self, you wished me luck and we parted our ways.

Was that it? I could not bring myself to think that I might never see you again. I held you in sight for a long time after you left, watching you walk on the curb, hail a cab, getting in, hoping against hope that you would give me one last glance before leaving.

When you did, I left with a bigger-than-ever gulp in my throat.

Goodbye

Dearest Aarav,

As I wait in the airport lounge for my flight – which is in the next two hours – I can't help but wish things had ended differently between us.

However, I was lucky to have found love in you. And so, while I am leaving in your absence, I do not wish to leave you blindsided any more than I already have.

I am leaving this rather long note (or in fact a eulogy) hoping you will find the answers to your questions about my decisions and actions. And I hope you can forgive me for not fulfilling our promise of ever-after.

Love,

Anya

GOODBYE

Dearest Yohan,

As I wait in the airport lounge for my flight – which is in the next one hour – I can't help but wish things had ended differently between us.

However, I was lucky to have found my life partner in you. And so, while I am leaving in you once again, I do not wish to leave you blindsided any more than I already have.

I am leaving this rather long note (or in fact a eulogy) hoping you will find the answers to your questions about my decisions and actions. And I hope you can forgive me for not fulfilling our promise of ever-after.

Love,

Anya

EPILOGUE

Five Years Later…

Anya was baking a chocolate cake in the kitchen. Her daughter was sitting on the counter, excited to reach the stage where she could do the piping on it with the icing cone. This was supposed to be her birthday gift to her daddy.

Anya had never imagined she would be getting another chance at starting her family after she left India. When she moved to London, she thought she had left behind all the courage she had to search for and strive for love. She was hopeless and hapless.

Life was difficult, especially when she thought back of all that she had left behind and all that she had destroyed. All she had wanted at that point was to find some respite in her work, and hence, she had drowned herself in work by taking up more than she could fit in her kitty.

She still wondered often how life could have been so miraculous as to bless her with so much love in one lifetime…

Miraya ran down to her daddy as he returned home from work that evening. She handed her daddy a happy-birthday card she had hand-written in her tiny scribbles with the new crayon set her mom had bought her. The card read,

Dearest Daddy,

Happy birthday to you.

You are the best daddy in the world. I love you.

- Miraya

Miraya's daddy received one more card that day – this one from Miraya's mom. It read,

My dear love,

Wish you a very happy birthday.

I thank my stars for bringing you in my life. And I thank you for following me to London five years ago. You taught me what love is. You taught me to not let the hurdles on the road to love break the journey, even though they may slow it down. You taught me that love is selfless, that it is not searching for happiness for the self, but it is finding that joy in your loved one's happiness. Thank you for finding me.

Most importantly, thank you for our lovely daughter – our precious treasure.

I Love You.

– Anya.